MORNINGSTAR

Book Three-
The Guardians of Truth

MORNINGSTAR

Book Three-
The Guardians of Truth

ONDI LAURE

Book cover design by www.jetlaunch.net
Book interior design by www.digitalcc.us

Follow Ondi Laure: https://MyInkLinks.com

Published by Story Launcher LLC: http://storylauncher.com
ISBN-13: 978-1-951451-23-3 (EPUB)
ISBN-13: 978-1-951451-22-6 (Perfect-Bound)

Scriptures taken from The Gnostic Society Library © 1995-2005
Lance Owens and The Bible Manuscript Society © 2013-2019

Disclaimer: Morningstar is a work of historical fiction. All names and characters are either invented or used fictitious. Any resemblance to actual persons is coincidental. To the best of the author's experience (her brush with death and her visit to an alternate dimension), heaven and our earthly realm are close. Moreover, while many events described in this book are historically accurate, God's boundless totality of being feminine, Sophia as much as being masculine, Jesus has yet to be authentically represented in historical scripture

I Dedicate This Book to My Sons

"What is hidden from you I will proclaim to you."

The Gospel of Mary 5:7

Table of Contents

BOOK III

CHAPTER ONE

Burial Arrangement

Charles found the room warm and cozy, though dusty, free of the evils that barraged his every ghostly stanza beyond the walls. Charles played in Saren's dreams a gentle melody for his daughter and the tiny life to which she so desperately clung. Though he played of spirit and health, no tears could grace his angelic face for the loss she would soon endure.

Charles played a sweet lullaby for Saren, as he had years past, to ensure her dreams were sweet.

◆　　◆　　◆

William and his mother carried Saren to the only straw mattress in their home. Ma laid Saren's legs upon the bed and unbound her laced boots, letting them drop to the dirt floor.

William was at the swaddled cloth Saren held so tightly in one swoop. He unwrapped the child to tend him.

His dread harnessed him. He clutched the dry, brittle cloth and whispered as he shivered. "Ma, come."

Together, William and his mother unswaddled the lifeless being. The tiny limbs clutched to the cloth. Both looked to Saren, envious of her ignorant slumber.

Ma, though, could feel the anguish and could not control her crying. It began for the infant's sake, though soon it changed to tears for the mother's loss. She did what any grieving mother would do and cleaned and cared for the tiny body as if it were her own departed flesh.

"We shan't remove the baby before Saren wakens," William consoled. "Once she wakens, I will go and arrange for his burial." With his hand upon his mother's shoulder, he retold the story of Saren's passage. "She searches for her Pa as I do, Ma. The girl was seen talking with the mute Jon just before his arrest." Gasping for a breath, he whispered, "Jon the Mute gave her a package. I watched." Wringing his hands, he continued, "The babe, she only found a few days back in a ransacked village. He is not her child, though she treated him as such."

"Ah-hhh", Ma gasped. "Dear child". Ma continued to rock the bundled, still, and quiet babe.

Saren's dreams went on and on. Throughout the night, she tossed and turned in her bed. Only once did she startle the whole house with her screams. She never woke until dawn when she reached for the infant near her bed. Her father's pipe music woke her as he gently carried little Liam from her dreams.

With no cradle nearby, Saren leaped from her slumber, disoriented. She gained her bearings as best she could recollect. Scanning the room for hints of her belongings, Saren's immediate need to relieve herself became more urgent; a chamber pot was now her priority.

"My, my," spoke William's ma as she rushed into the room. "Good day, young lady. I am glad ye are awake. A wild and fearful night ye had. The torment you must have been through," Ma offered the remains of her weary smile. "Are ye well, my child?"

"Oh, why, yes. My night was fine. This was the first night we have slept in a warm bed with a roof upon us for many moons' cycles. Why would I not be?" Saren's attention was now on searching for wee Liam.

"You slept a frightful night, filled with screams and cries, that is all," William explained from behind the open door.

Saren did not seem troubled by this news and went about looking and fidgeting.

"I've bathed the poor child and swaddled him plenty. Yet no nourishment will help em now." Looking at Saren, Ma held open her hands. "Come child, what horrors ye have seen." Ma pulled Saren snugly into her strong arms with a warm hug. "Please call me Ma. Everyone does."

Saren's eyes filled with tears. "I have not had a mother's embrace in many moons. Thank you," she whispered, though barely audible.

"William, we need some other supplies from the market. Now move along, lad, an make the burial arrangement ye must."

William gathered his coat and purse yet tossed his cap to the side. Giving Saren a knowing nod, he hastened away.

The silence between the women was natural, for no words were necessary. They spoke seldom and then only about Liam and what his tiny being had brought to them both. They drank ale and ate the remaining pottage.

Saren caught her breath once, realizing William had been away too long. She also realized Ma was unaware that she and her son were being searched for.

Ma took heed of the worry that suddenly appeared in Saren's expression. She stood and stepped to the shut window, cracking it open enough to peer into the street. "He'll be along, my dear. No need to worry. He's a good lad, my William." Returning to the table, Ma sipped from her goblet before sitting. "Unless, of course, ye know a reason for trouble to find him," Ma said more than she asked.

Saren could not escape Ma's deep gaze; her blue eyes begged for truth. She loathed keeping one secret from this dear woman who had shown her nothing but kindness and respect.

Saren closed her eyes as if searching for the precise moment the events began to unfold. Events that led her here to be having a meal at this aged alder table, worrying about the whereabouts of her new friend's son, William. *The beginning is a fine place to start, I presume.* Saren cleared her throat with a deliberate cough. "I left my home as spring ended, yes—now what season is near, mid-summer?" She wiped her lips with the back of her hand as she began to tell her saga.

Saren spoke on into the day, never slowing her tale even when William returned. She only breathed a sigh and continued.

Ma rose and began taking provisions from the larder. She was churning butter as Saren told of her flight from the angry crowd with William. Saren finally rose to find the satchel the mute, Jon, had given her. She emptied its contents upon the table.

Four books of varying sizes wrapped and bound in soft leather straps lay on the table. "Bibles?" Saren clasped her hand over her mouth. "We have partially translated Wycliffe Bibles, Will? The book of … I cannot say."

CHAPTER TWO

Rules of Men

Scanning the room, Saren needed to occupy her restless hands. She tore tiny bites from the bread loaf as tears escaped her eyes. The realization of losing her little Liam fell upon her. Ma came to stand near her. "I know, my child, ye are but a girl, and still ye cared for this lad as if he was yer own." Ma draped her arm across Saren's trembling shoulders. "Ye are a good mother. Liam knows all ye have done for him."

With this, Saren began to cry. "No, I should have found him food sooner." She sobbed now over the baby. "And all for a sack of mostly Latin books that I can not even read!" Saren's sobs of shame burst like claps of thunder.

"Saren, Ma. Come now!" William calmly took them from the open window and shut the clapboards. "They are searching for us. The books are neither ours nor belong to those seeking them." William stood tall over the table, losing his boyish charm. "I do not know what these books are or what they say. There are guards everywhere outside." He looked to his Ma. "Jon the Mute knew. He was a friend of Pa's, and he knew where Pa was, too." Will began to pace the floor. "This is all connected to Pa's disappearance! I know it," he proclaimed.

Saren wiped her tear-streaked face before coming to the table. She carefully unbound the fourth bundled book. They examined it as if it were precious art—the pages unmarked and pure, the ink and writing fresh and new.

I think I know someone who can read us these pages," William whispered.

Saren traced the letters with the tips of her fingers, making sounds where she thought they ought to be. "I am not come to call the right…" Her furrowed brow only deepened as she tried to decipher the Latin words.

Ma encouraged her. "Keep trying the words, Saren. You are doing fine. Where did you learn this?"

Smiling at the memory, Saren spoke of her father. "Father believed wisdom to be the answer to everything. He would read to me each night from Dante Alighieri's poems in Latin. "Father believed, 'Idolatry would hasten our demise'." As her strong fingers turned the leaves of the book, a loose paper sealed with wax fell to the floor. "Thou shalt," Saren read. "The writing is different here—it looks like a letter signed by Jon."

"That is his mark. Yes, that is Jon the Mute's mark. I saw that when I brought his messages for Pa." Will crossed his arms over his chest as he paced, stopping near the door to look at his ma and then at Saren. "These books are what the soldiers want." Will unfolded his arms and let them drop to his sides. Stepping to the table, he reached for one of the unwrapped Bibles. "What did the people call Jon, Saren? When they took him away?"

"Lollard, a Lollard, Will. But the Church has now made this a negative title." Saren could not follow his thoughts. With her chin held at an angle, she gave Will a questioning stare and added, "With King Richard's rein, Father was proud to be one of the Lollard Knights."

William stood tall over the books spread across the table. "These English translations oppose the Church, Saren." He nodded to the books.

Saren sighed and closed her eyes to the candle's glow. "My father, too, was a Lollard. Jon the Mute was to help me here in London," she closed the book. Reaching for another, she added, "Jon was to take me to the priest at St. Othy's Cathedral."

Her every fiber tingled with suspicion of where her father's secret books, which beckoned from within her satchel, fit into this ever-growing puzzle. She kept her secret.

Ma rose and began walking about the small room. "Your pa would know of this; he never said, though. I believe he was helping the Lollards in his deliveries to Jon." She covered her face with her hands to hide her tears.

"Why? Why does the Church want them? The Church does not want the people to read the Bible in English?" Saren gnawed her lip. "I've got some more studying to do. We will learn to read them for ourselves.

"We must get rid of the books. Why do we have to have them in this home?" Ma asked, still weeping.

Will rose to stand next to the table. Bracing his young frame with outstretched hands across the smoothed, worn table's surface, he spoke. "Ma, I understand your fears. We can't get rid of the books yet, for maybe they will lead us to Pa." He looked toward Saren as she rose.

"Will, the Church does not want the people to hear God's word in a language they understand. The Church then loses its power, its control over the people," Saren said. Her eyes met Will's across the table in the candle's glow.

Reading the first book served as a welcome distraction for Saren. She had not yet grown accustomed to being without little Liam, and now her tender heart resisted the day's dawning. Saren kept to her task of reading and studying the Latin text. Elaborate as the writing was, she understood quickly, having read many times with her father.

"This I did understand from the Book of Matthew: 'I am not come to call the righteous...'" Saren nodded in thought. "This short phrase reveals all the hypocrisy of the Church... It is no wonder that the English Crown, France, and Rome would only want these words shared in Latin. No wonder only a few elites and rich are taught this language, as the righteous are not being called by God."

"Ma, was the Church as strong when you were a girl? Will asked. "When do you imagine this all began to be accepted?"

"My mother and father knew no other church. It has always been taught so." Ma was silent then as she concentrated on the past. "How can we have been blinded to truth many generations to witness a holy suppression as this?" she reasoned, sitting across the table from Saren.

"Ma, few in this kingdom have ever listened to the Bible read in anything but Latin. How do we know what it says? We only know what the Church tells us to be true." Saren looked to William for help, knowing from the days she spent traveling the road with her father that poverty and suffering succeeded among the oppressed.

"Ma, look at the villages nearby. We are all poor, working, starving. Then there are the royals, the bishops, the clergy. They are all rich and fashionable." He paused and continued, "We are told to pay for the price of our sin during collection each Sunday, right? If we don't go to Church, we must pay twice for our sin of not being present." William looked at his mother. "We are not the sinners here, Ma. The clergy and the Crown are. They are stealing from us and using the word of God and his book to do so."

With a shaking sigh, Ma agreed. "The oppression is unjust and evil; you two are the chosen to have happened upon these books." Ma reached for Saren's hand. "Can you write well enough to make more copies of these Bibles to spread them about the kingdom? Would you dare take such a risk? The ultimate price is our lives." Her voice shook.

"But Ma." William hesitated. "People can't read them."

"No, Will. Many people cannot, now. But some can. And we will find them."

Saren rose to retrieve her belongings but hesitated, saying, "Like Wycliffe's followers, he first wrote the Bible's verses in English. He, John Wycliffe, is the first-morning star of this dawning." Sitting back in her seat at the table, Saren told all that she could remember. "My father was outwardly an obedient churchman. He always appeared accepting and true, but he knew the true scheme of the Church, though he never spoke ill of the Church. He always made me act my very best and pay our collection when we could." Saren rubbed her straining eyes. "Father always spoke of a good God, a Lord, unlike the Roman Church. My mother's mother, my Nan, she hated the Church. Feuded with them, in fact. She would tell Father, 'I'm too ill to come to Mass. I haven't the strength for their hate!' I wish I'd paid more mind to her views before, but I was just a child." Saren paced the floor where Will had been walking. "My Nan was raised Pagan, of course." Saren's smile wavered as she spoke of her grandmamma. "She isn't a witch, but the people of the Church all spoke of her as such. Perhaps she is." Saren's smile returned. "Father told her time and again, 'We have no other choice but to do as the Crown says.'" Saren slumped upon her seat. "Nan called my father a coward then."

"He wasn't a coward, Saren. He was wise. No one can fight the Church. They have been in power too long."

Saren stood near the closed door as if expecting company to arrive, as she continued recollecting her grandmamma's words. "She wasn't a witch, though she knew things through her prayers and chants. She could see things before any of us." Deep in thought, she quietly paced. "Ma, Will, it is not just the Romans, now. Look who the Church has become: the entire royal court, The King, his soldiers, his council, the ministries, their wives, their children, the bishops. Nan worried then for my father; his greatest weakness was believing that he alone could save the people from the Church's disguise, though he respected the power of what he opposed."

"We feed them. We pay for our collection even when we cannot afford cream to make our butter. They do nothing but make laws and rules based on a false doctrine." William's face turned the color of fire and appeared hot to the touch.

Saren paced the dirt floor, remembering Joseph's readings upon the AL-Aoura words from the Coptic Gospel of Mary, *'Do not lay down any rules beyond what I appointed you.'* [1]

"Yes, William… I mean Will. These are the rules of men. Not of Christ Jesus."

"No wonder Pa is gone. He and Jon were onto this. What were they going to do, I wonder?" William rubbed his chin between his thumb and finger as his pa would have. "We must see if Jon's cart remains in the square." Holding his breath, Will paused nearer the fire. "Saren, would you dare join me?" he asked as he exhaled.

"My Nan was right that my father alone couldn't help the people and spread the true word of God." Saren silently recalled her Nan's prayer and realized that something far grander than English Bibles was threatening the Church—the threat she carried in her satchel. "We, together, are a great force, are we not?"

Ma jumped to a protective stance. "Nay, Saren, girl. You are being looked for, my dear," she said protectively. "Ye see, it is just that…" Ma fumbled for the right words. "You will stand out. Yer appearance is striking enough that people notice, my child. And the two of you together, well, people will take heed."

"You are right, Ma. We must take special care to not make ourselves known." Looking about the room, Saren added, "And we need a plan, a pact to go by if one of us were to be taken." The shared gaze between Will and his ma revealed their intent. "Then we won't get caught. And if we do, we die trying to share the truth."

"Pa risked, Pa sacrificed himself, Ma, for these books." Will shook his head and rocked himself back and forth. "I must learn their true meaning with Saren before I am to do the same. Before I risk you, Ma, or you, Saren, going to prison for something we know little about." Will knew deep in his gut what must be done—and done at any cost. Yet he could not help but voice his concerns again.

CHAPTER THREE

The Bridge from Heaven

A knock came at the door, sending the trio hustling to gather the books. Sweeping them carefully together, Ma wrapped them all snugly in an elegantly embroidered bed slip and laid them at the foot of the straw-filled bed.

Saren stood over the kitchen's flame, rocking. William grabbed his cap and stuffed her long, wild hair deep within it, then secured it atop her head before he answered the door with much cheer.

"Aye, lad. I have a message for you and your mother from the courts here." The fat man fumbled through his tablet to read, "Your pa, your husband, is being held for conspiracies to heresy is due for execution come July." The soldier turned to leave, not expecting a reply.

William lowered his head and dragged his fingers through his flaxen yellow hair. Squinting his eyes, he scowled at the man through his gnarled teeth with a witty protest. "What? Arrested for heresy, you tell? He has been away for weeks. My ma has been worried to death. We do not have money for food or provisions, let alone recourse to your accusations, and you come to tell us such nonsense. My Pa has done nothing of the sort." William stood square, his shoulders thrust forward, a hand locked on each hip.

"You'd best watch your sass, or you too will join him at Oxford Prison." The guard thrust his hands to his own hips. "Now, I best advise you t… to… go find work for your family, B… Boy…" the fat man stammered, turned, and strolled away.

"Heresy? Hmm. Will that be what they call our crimes," Ma jested. "We need supplies: pens, ink, paper, food." She returned to the shuttered window to watch the guard meandering up the street. "What do we do first? I wish we could talk to Pa. He'd know what we are to do." Ma began to hum an old melody as she prepared a meal of bread and broth.

"What do you sing, Ma? I recognize your tune." Saren began to hum along and soon sang words to her father's ballad.

> *"The drivers through the woodès went [All] for to raise the deer,*
>
> *Bowmen bicker'd upon the bent With their broad arrows clear.*
>
> *Then the wild° thoro' the woodès went On every sidè shear;*
>
> *Grayhounds thoro' the grevès glent For to kill their deer.*

This began on Cheviot the hills abune Early on a Monenday;

By that, it drew to the hour of noon. A hundred fat harts dead there lay."[2]

Saren shut her eyes and could hear his pipes from the beach singing along. William snarled at the women, "Ladies, must we? This is no time for song. We have serious business at stake. Pa's life, perhaps."

"No, listen, Will. Your ma is singing a border ballad. I know the words. Many of the ballads came from pagan songs my Nan often sang. And for this reason, she would try to accept the Church…" Saren's eyes were shut as she mouthed the words of the ballad. Saren added, "My Nan was mean. Not evil, just bitter, and sometimes ornery to my father. It was only the three of us then since Mother had passed. Nan blamed Pa for their deaths, I reckon, looking back on it. Pa also did because he could not save them. Nan never really liked my father so much, but they had me to raise between them, and I was all that either of them had. They did their best." Saren smiled at the happy memories.

"Nan refused the Church, though it was one more thing she could fight Father over. She was pagan and refused to change her beliefs. Grandmamma would tell me oft that the Church, Christendom, was the Roman man's Church, not for the wise Gaelic women. 'We can't be fooled,' she would laugh. 'I seek my own path to unity of the divine, not some man's.'" Smiling, Saren went on. "Nan drank mead like the ancient Egyptians and laughed at my girlish naivete. She could have been a pirate or a witch herself in a past life, by the stories she would tell. 'I hate for you, my Saren girl, to grow up and marry into repression as your mother did.'" Saren smiled, "I don't know why she believed my mother was repressed. I always knew my mother was happy and in love with my father. Nan would sing and play on her flute songs of love and life, songs of God, of heaven, of nature. They were songs and Psalms from the Old Testament, too. Nan knew God's love; she shared it in her music. She would sit upon the shores and play to the tempo of the falling waves, and then there were the days that she would play to the swelling of them. Either way, the music came from the depths of her soul like magic." Lost in thought, Saren's eyes cleared with realization. "Just as my father's did. His music was his bridge to heaven, to my mother. Father played his pipes; they would play together, Nan and him. They would play into the night. There were nights that their magic would sing me to sleep and then wake me again at dawn with their sweet lullaby. They fought colossally, the pair of them. If there was music to be shared, it kept them civil, reminded them that there was humanness between them besides raising me." Saren's shoulders slumped, drained from the weight of the memory, though comforted in knowing that now her father's music was his bridge to her from heaven.

"'Faith,' she would tell, 'is my freedom. My God holds no strings to me, no purse. Why, then, would I choose a God of greed and restraint? My God is pure, nature, all around.' Her God was in her every thought and song, upon each note from her flute, not found in a building before a throne, nor bartered for." Saren sat back in her chair, crossing her arms upon her breast. "You see, Nan has wisdom like no one else. Perhaps that was one reason the town believed she was a witch." She looked to Ma but would not look William in the eye. There was something awkward about telling him, directly, her ancient family secret.

"Nan knew about things to happen. She knew before me that I was leaving her for this quest. We sang Psalms from the Old Testament that day on the stony shore. Now I understand what she was preparing me for." Saren continued to hum her grandmamma's prayer:

"Come to me with your powers, and howsoever I may use them, may they have good success and to whomsoever I may give them. Whatever grant, it may prosper."[3]

CHAPTER FOUR

A Backfired Plan

The sun had not peered through the vast sky since Saren and her tiny baby Liam had arrived in London on Midsummer's Eve. William's suspicion of Jon, the mute's, involvement with his father's arrest prompted him to be near the city center the day Saren arrived in London. And now the unraveling mystery could not be stopped.

"The rain is letting up; shall we run for Jon's cart? That is where Father exchanged letters to be carried far. Someone continues to pass messages from there, but who?" Will asked as he led the way.

The cap slipped loose from Saren's hair as they neared Jon's rickety old cart. An older man dressed in fine linen, wearing a woolen scarf, stooped to retrieve it from the mud. "Why hide your glorious locks beneath that old thing?" he asked as he handed the cap to Saren.

She nodded and gave her best curtsy.

Hurrying on ahead, William caught his breath, not noticing the old man watching him unlatch the trap door beneath the belly of the old cart where Jon stashed letters and writing supplies.

They had been noticed. Saren diverted her eyes and stepped behind Will. The man watched the suspicious pair for one more moment and then left. Will nearly choked, "Keep moving past the cart." Without taking a breath, he added, "There are things left there. It looks like the cart is being watched. We can't have him notice us snooping about here." He gave her a gentle push. "Keep moving, Saren."

Braiding her hair quickly, Saren rolled the hair rope into a bun and refastened it into the cap. "There, that shan't happen again." Looking back toward the cart, she asked, "Shall we go back?"

"Yes, the trap door had been opened, and there was something placed inside. One of us must stand guard. Can you whistle?"

She gave a loud, shrill whistle through her teeth. "Perfect." Taking a deep breath, William said, "Let's give it a go."

Saren strolled from street to street, looking at the pretty things to buy as if she had any money. Pretty people wearing pretty clothes passed by. No one spoke to her or paid her much mind. This troubled her and made her feel small, though she was glad not to receive any unwanted attention. Recognizing a tall, thinner man in the market looking more at the people than the goods offered. Saren recognized him at first glance and nearly hollered his name in recognition.

Terror flooded her mind, and the realization of the significance of his presence here in London shook her. Lord Percy was looking upon each face among London's inhabitants. Being uncertain of his son's, Sir Percy's, identity, Saren was confident that they both were now in London looking for her.

Tucking the loose curls that had fallen from her braid beneath her cap and pulling Pa Wynch's scarf across her neck to conceal herself, she turned her back as she departed the city's center, knowing well that her father's book was no longer safe within these city's walls. She was bumped from behind as she stood waiting for Will with enough force that she lost her footing upon the muddy street and toppled into it.

A father's greatest fear is of his daughter finding a husband, a lover, or a man appealing. Charles had seen it happening when Saren had ridden, babe in her arms, behind Percy's son on the horse. Charles did not have much room for concern then, for Saren was so weak from exhaustion and hunger along her journey to London.

Her attraction to the knight, however, was natural. Charles could not physically intervene nor control his daughter falling for a man. A traitor's son. But from his ethereal purgatory, he could get in the way.

Charles pulled his pipes out and played a lively reel close to a young man's head, hoping he would leap away, knocking Saren's admirer further into the crowd.

His plan backfired as the young lad apparently approved of the reel. He jumped forward with a jig, knocking Saren's suitor into her, sending her to her rump, and Charles dipped into the mud.

⬧　⬧　⬧

"Good heavens, my lady." the man, now dressed in King Henry's colors, stooped to Saren's aid. "How clumsy I am. Let me help you." He grasped her hands in his own and pulled her into his clutch. Not intentionally, though his build was large and hers just tiny, the knighted man of the court pulled her with excessive gusto, perhaps fueled slightly by his pride. But once there in his arms, he recognized her. Their eyes met for an instant. He asked, "How is your babe, My Lady?" He dropped her gaze. "You appear to have found your family here in London."

Saren smiled but could not speak. She bobbed her head and breathed in his smell, remembering the muscles she had wrapped her arms around as he brought Liam and her to London.

Without notice, William slipped behind her and grabbed her forearm.

"Oh! You startled me," she said.

"Sorry, come now. I've gotten it. Let's hurry home," Will whispered.

Saren smiled at the guard. "My brother needs to run along. Have a good day, sir." She blushed and hurried off with William.

"Take the long route, Will." Saren screwed up her face in embarrassment. "We mustn't attract more notice." She attempted to wipe the stains off her soiled skirt. They hurried for home but grabbed one another occasionally when the pace became too alarming. They raced for home, presumably unobserved.

From the opposite side of the city center, a man with graying eyebrows had watched the young couple as they left the square. He noticed the young bright-eyed lad again as he stole something from the belly of Jon the mute's abandoned cart. He raised his arm in alarm to holler but was startled by a loud crash behind him. He turned to look before he jumped from the path of a tower of crashing crates. When he turned back, the kids were gone. He shrugged and went to locate the king's knight he had seen exchange words with the black-haired girl.

❖   ❖   ❖

CHAPTER FIVE

Secrets

They burst into Ma's kitchen, welcomed by the familiar smell of simmering pottage. Both turned in relief to each other at the success of making it to their home.

"Ahoy, the house!" William shouted. Ma came hurrying at once.

"Thank goodness. I have been so fearful!" Ma rushed to her son.

He let her hug him before removing his load of packages. "Look here, Ma. We now have paper. And here is ink!" he said with a grin like a pirate's, having found a treasure.

"Splendid, Will. The ink is worth a fortune." Saren leaped to examine one of her books. "Look here, this paper matches many of the one Bible's pages." She waited for another to speak.

"Aye, Saren. Jon then must have written these pages."

"Yes, Ma," William agreed. "Where had Pa been the last day that we saw him?" he changed the subject.

"He had come from Otterburn the day before and left for London's St. Osyth's Cathedral at dawn. Not to be heard of until this week." Tears welled again in Ma's eyes. "Excuse me, children." Realizing her husband's guilty affiliation with transcribing and distributing the forbidden English Bibles, she rose and started toward her bedchamber, saying, "If Pa is found guilty, they may keep him in prison. They may sentence him to death!"

William rushed to his ma.

Ma's bedchambers smelled of lye soap and stale air. For one so small of frame, Ma's bed rose twice her size in height. No tokens of her person adorned the nightstand, and only one ragged housecoat hung from a wooden peg. No light penetrated the room, for there were no windows. A lone candle sat on the nightstand.

Will sat upon the straw bed beside his ma. The lad's weight caused the bed of hay to sag. He draped his arm around his ma's small back.

"There, there, Ma. I feel your pain and know your worry. But we must keep our wits." Will squeezed her shoulders softly. Choking back tears of his own, he continued. "Ma, look how fortunate we are to have found Saren. Look what joy and hope she brings to our small home." William lit the candle and held it as he watched the flame dance. Mesmerized, he watched the wax begin to drip, and the flame grow, and with it, his spirit.

His voice, calm initially, echoed through the dingy walls made of straw and mud. His anger began to erode the hope he may have once had from their day's success. William's fears were real and honest. No boy ought to lose a father without a fight.

The kitchen grew dark. Saren rose to light lamps to brighten her own spirits. Curious about the day's discoveries, she searched deeper into the satchels for the pen Jon had used. She was not confident in writing things so precious, even if just copying.

Saren removed the loot tenderly from the blanket in which it was wrapped. She also found where William had tucked Jon's letter.

Opening Jon the Mute's letter, Saren began to decipher it. The writing was clear and legible. She had no trouble reading the words or making sense of their meaning. Still, she could not keep her eyes from wandering back to her family's secrets that she would take to St. Osyth's Cathedral, just as William's father had done.

Saren touched the sacred book. Her hands lingered there, feeling the dry leather that bound them. Her heart yearned to open them, to remember what she had heard Joseph read upon the Al-Auora.

The second book bound, Saren tried translating from her Coptic gift and the only work that she had done months past. She again embarked upon her journey of divination. She read her notes, '*The seven powers of wrath,*' was the final conversation Mary wrote in her Gospel before the other disciples questioned the savior speaking with a woman and not them. Searching through the document,

Saren located the first form as darkness. She contemplated this correlation to the time at hand and the darkness that began to loosen its grip.

The demon of disillusionment, weariness, discouragement, defeat beckoned at their door. Saren marked her reading of her family's secret book well for safekeeping and further study before grabbing her heart and trusting with all her might that her light was shining past the darkness, darkness that reigned supreme for generations. With a flicker of the candle's flame and a shift of her books upon the table, a letter fell to the floor.

> *Dear Jon,*
>
> *This being the completion of John Wycliffe's works from 1380, I am enlisting his aid for additional transcribers as I start to work on the Apostle John's final book, Revelations.*
>
> *I shall return with news of it in one month. Rev. John Sautrey*
>
> *St. Michael's*
>
> *Coventry*

"There, that is it. Ma, Will, I've got it." Saren rushed to Ma's bedside. "The letter explains it. The books were transcribed by John Wycliffe. The letter, I presume, was written to our Jon at the cart by a third John. John Sautrey."

Wide-eyed, Saren exclaimed, "We must find this John Sautrey. The Father mentions one more book that is being translated from Latin." *And I will deliver my treasures and be rid of their burden,'* Saren thought.

"How will we find this man, this Reverend Sautrey?" Ma asked. "He writes that he will return to assist Jon in one month. We must figure out when that will be and make contact," Saren declared.

"I hope, Saren, all of yer and William's efforts will bring Pa home sooner." Small tears pooled in Ma's blue eyes. "I wish for the both of ye to go to Coventry immediately and speak with Father Sautrey."

"Ma, how on earth will we pay for our passage? We have no money," Saren said, her father's book on her mind. Imagining she would give them to Father Sautrey and be rid of this burden at last filled her with relief. She found a smile despite her slumped shoulders.

Ma said, "If we can clear Pa's name and get him home, there is no cost, nor trial, that I wouldn't pay to try." Her tears fell from her face and splashed upon her fairylike hands. "I have some treasured silver to be sold. We will send William to market first thing. Now, you need some rest." Ma patted Saren's hand with her own, wet with her tears, but a gentle knock at their door sent each into their own panic.

CHAPTER SIX

Crimes of The Heart

Sir Henry Percy brought her to London on the day of King Henry IV's coronation. Security had been heightened. His father, Lord Percy, had commanded him to hurry back to the front line immediately after depositing the itinerant girl and her infant from the back of his galloping horse at the gates of London.

He later regretted not asking her name. The sparkle in her eye as he left her there upon the packed earth as he rode away haunted him still.

Now, after having brushed into her on the street only three days before and sending her to the mud, he'd been a bristle of nerves. Here he—Sir Henry Percy II, the gallant knight—was, walking around the city, pushing ladies down in the mud.

Sir Henry Percy came from the elite Percy family of Northumberland.

Lord Percy, his father, had slipped through the cracks into the next king's reign of power. It was not usual for a king to retain a knight from the preceding sovereign regime. Lord Percy was the pawn of evil-doing and was often in opportune situations for self-gain. His father's involvement in the fall of King Richard, thus aligning events for Henry Bolingbroke's assumption of the Crown, meant that Sir Henry Percy was also granted a place among the new nobility.

Sir Percy returned to the barracks after walking from his mother's home. Though married, she lived alone and triumphantly, away from his father's vices. His mind was elsewhere, as it had been now for days. He rounded the corner and entered the foyer gate when the guardsmen took him by each arm. Grabbing him firmly, nearly penetrating his coat with their grip, they escorted him into the building.

"May I ask what this is all about, Lads?" Sir Percy asked, knowing too well that they could not speak to him without a witness. He then teased, "Is this a joke? What seems to be troubling you?" They didn't answer his questions. He remained quiet and went with his friends compliantly.

They took him to the Tower of London for questioning. In the dark, dank room sat the bishop, his closest clergyman, and a soldier, along with his superior officer, the highest-ranked knight of the king's court, Lord Beauchamp. Sir Percy stood just inside the door, watching the men around the table, but refrained from speaking until he was summoned.

"Good day, Sir Percy," uttered his superior. "I'm sure you have questions concerning your arrest, but first, we must ask you some questions." The man motioned for him to sit among the others at the table.

He stepped forward, not frightened but concerned. His forehead was creased in the center. He sat across from the bishop's protégé.

"Where were you on the seventh day of this month, Sir Percy?" The lord questioned.

"I was working, Sir. Here at the court and then on assignments around the city," Henry said, looking around at the men in the room. He knew all the men-at-arms but did not recognize the man dressed in church clothes beside the bishop.

Reverend Dudley stood, a grouchy-looking man with graying hair and eyebrows. "What you were doing that day in the street, laying in the mud with… with… with that girl?"

The men all looked at Sir Percy for his answers. He did not answer, though. For a moment, he, too, turned red, as his poor conduct had worried him for days. As he prepared to answer, he doubted the reverend's intentions, and looking to Lord Beauchamp, Sir Percy replied, "I was on duty, Sir. The streets were filled with mud. I heard a loud noise, and a lad was dancing a Jig upon the planked walk, knocking me into a young girl and sending her into the street, Sir." Sir Percy scanned his peers for their reaction. Two of them had smiles masked behind clasped hands. Reverend Dudley rose to his feet.

"Well, you know the girl. I saw you speak to her. She must have given you her name. Now, I demand to know it," the gray-eyebrowed man spat bitterly.

"Is she a criminal, Father? Should I have arrested her for something, Sir?" Sir Percy locked eyes with the Priest.

"I watched that boy and her steal things from the old, abandoned cart in the square. They are up to something." He wiped saliva from his mouth with his sleeve. "She was disguised—she was hiding her hair. She lost her cap, a boy's cap, and she thrust her hair back into it." The Priest diverted his eyes. She's the girl we searched for after Jon the Mute was seized. An ally of the Lollards, she has Jon's Lollard Bibles. I know it!" Sweat collected upon the Priest's forehead despite the coolness of the room.

Sir Percy collaborated, for neither he, the bishop, nor anyone else in the room knew she was Saren Eadwine of Northumberland, Sir Percy's betrothed.

Lord Beauchamp spoke up, "Thank you, Father. Would you and Sir Percy compile a thorough description of this girl for our record? If she is spotted again, we will arrest her and have you come in to identify her." The captain turned to face Sir Percy. "In the meantime, Sir. Would you please find her identity and place of residence? Then we may make a formal arrest."

Sir Percy stood to look the Priest directly in the eye once more. "What charge do we bring the girl in for, Sir." He directed his question toward his captain.

The Priest, though, reiterated his case. "Heresy! Arrest her for heresy," he demanded and stomped from the room.

The knights of the court, the armsman, and Sir Henry Percy all sat in the cheerless room, waiting for someone else to speak. At last, Sir Percy stood, saying, "Sir, the father did not describe the girl. I will do my best to help." He gave the bishop a respectful bow and a nod and walked from the room.

Sir Henry pictured her eyes perfectly in his mind; her lips, rosy and moist, beckoned to be kissed. Her hair, a toppled mass of waves and curls tucked beneath her boyish hat. He could draw her perfect portrait down to the most minute detail. That was his trouble; he couldn't get her out of his mind.

Yes, he wanted to know her name, wanted to know if this was his betrothed—but not to have her arrested. He silently prayed.

CHAPTER SEVEN

Coventry

The horses were harnessed, and the riders were waiting to depart for Coventry when Saren and William arrived at the stable. The cart was loaded with dry goods for merchants along the road and in Coventry. Saren and William carried in their satchel a slice of bread wrapped in cloth, a pouch of mead, and a few coins between them. Saren secured the obsidian blade she'd fashioned from stone, saying, "I wish we had a bow. I remember my father left me arrows for my journey, though there was never time to build a bow. Now, how I wish that I'd made the time." She sighed.

Nonetheless, the escorts were armed, carrying swords at their hips and arrows across their backs. Though their bows were small, they hung from their saddles, readily accessible.

William was the first to clamber upon the cart. Once seated, he beckoned. "Well, are you coming or not? We haven't all day. The horses are eager to move."

Saren looked at the prancing cob-horses before sitting in the wagon beside William for their journey to deliver English Bibles and Saren imagined, *her family's secret books,* to Father Sautrey.

Despite the wooden wheels, the cart was quick and smooth with the rapid clip of the horse's small hooves. Saren chuckled and bit her lip as she spoke of her ride into London behind the mounted knight. "Liam didn't wake up until we stopped," Saren remembered. She then added, "The horses smelled different than these." As she said the words, something else occupied her mind. Her face became flushed; she turned away.

The riders talked and goaded each other. They were young for the responsibility of protecting lives on the road. Saren watched, pained by their childishness. She thought out loud, "What I would give to have my father's bow and quiver today."

William looked to her for clarification. "What? Why?" he asked.

"For our protection, that is why." She pointed into the trees at a rider moving among the shadows. "They don't see him." Saren leaned forward upon her wooden seat and tapped the driver on the shoulder.

He sneered over his shoulder, "What, woman? Can't ye see et I'm busy?" His eyes returned to the road.

"Sir, there is a man ahead of us in the trees. Shan't you take heed?"

"What, man? I's sees no man, woman!" He spat upon her as he spoke.

Saren looked to William for assistance, but William had not seen the rider, so he only shrugged and said, "We have to trust these men, Saren."

"You mean, boys. William, these are not men." The party approached the tree line rapidly. Saren held her breath as the sun disappeared beyond the foliage, and she clutched her arms across her chest as the shade made her shiver. She held her breath as a man dressed in black sat upon a black horse in the middle of their path, his cloak pulled over his lower face. She grabbed for William's hand.

"Whoa, boys," the leading rider stammered. "Who do we have here? Good day to ya, Sir." The mounted rider rode past the cart, turned, and began following behind much slower.

Saren dared not look back. William tapped her on the arm, and she leaped to him. "He's following us, Saren."

"I imagine," she replied.

"Should we tell the driver?"

"He knows, Will." Saren held her breath.

They cleared the forest unscathed. When Saren finally took a good gulp of air, she turned to look behind them. The rider was gone. "Umph! Will, looks like we have been made the fools. I imagine that man works for these gents. Do you reckon? I'd call him their partner." She giggled. "The bandit in the trees keeps our guards employed. No doubt."

The driver turned and gave her a challenging look confirming her suspicions.

◆   ◆   ◆

Coventry was a small village compared to London; it was much cleaner and warmer. The people did not appear to be in such a rush as those in London. The friendliest merchants that Saren had ever spoken to were here. She had never been given notice or kindness from a stranger in London like that she received in Coventry.

They ate their bread and sipped ale before leaving the city's center. William asked about the church's location, and one small boy offered his services to take them safely to their destination.

However, Saren was flattered. She refused him in a gentle yet direct manner. William was angered by her refusal. "He was only being nice, Saren. You should have let him take us." He walked away, shaking his dirty blonde curls into the breeze.

"Will, he wasn't taking us for free. We were to pay him for his time. He was expecting one of our few coins. We can manage our way without payment." Saren shook her head and went after him.

The pair walked the clean streets. The air felt clear, and crisp compared to the smoke-filled air of London. "We must move here," Saren thought aloud as they neared St. Michael's cathedral.

There, before the gate, Will stopped and turned to his partner. "Shall we go in?" He swung the gate open.

The door to the church rose taller than their ceiling back home. Saren gawked upward at its vastness. This William also opened for her. They strode in together.

Candles were burning around the altar, illuminating colorful windows and paintings of Biblical fables. Covering her mouth with a hand, Saren soaked in the grandeur. The cathedral housed a grand chapel of white marble. The main foyer was separated on each side by a series of arches reaching higher than any tree Saren had ever seen. She stood motionless in the center of the room, frozen in wonderment.

William had to squeeze her hand as a young nun approached from the depths of the cathedral.

"Can I help you?" she asked.

"Yes," William spoke as Saren remained speechless.

The nun came closer, and a smile spread across her face. She laid a hand on Saren's shoulder. She followed her gaze to the portrait of Jesus on the wall, surrounded by brilliant colors. "It's magnificent, isn't it? The yellow and gold paint really is gold, don't you know," she told them.

"Why?" Saren asked. Does that make it more beautiful?"

The smile remained upon the friendly nun's lips. "Can I help you?" she repeated, dropping her hand from Saren's shoulder.

"Yes, I'm sorry," Saren muttered. "Forgive my rudeness, Sister." Saren looked at her feet. "I lost myself in it all." Saren looked to William once more for his help.

"Sister, my name is William Wynch of London." He gave a quiet bow of his head. "We have come to speak with Father Sautrey. Is he available today?"

"Very well. I will see." The dainty little woman spun on her heels and exited the room.

The cathedral walls echoed the quiet. Built of marble bricks, the walls kept the sounds beyond the glorious paintings from penetrating the church.

The aged hardwood floor glistened like clear black ice, free of one single blemish. Only the flutter of candles' flames gave any hint of life.

Saren and William dared not move and disturb the stillness; they waited. A flick of a door latch, and there he strode, walking to them from the depths of the cathedral.

A young-looking man, younger than a Roman Catholic priest ought to look, stopped before them without speaking.

William stepped forth; his hand poised for an introduction. He greeted the priest. "Good day, Father Sautrey. My name is William. William Wynch, Father." Will thrust his hand toward the man for him to shake. When the priest did not accept it, Will stuffed his hand into his pocket.

"How may I help you, children?" the priest leered. He, too, thrust his hands beneath his cassock.

"We've come from London to ask…" Saren looked to William for his expertise. She became more reluctant to hand over her family's precious sacred book. "We need your help, Father."

"And who may I ask is asking? For my help, that is." The priest's eyes remained on the girl.

"Oh, my Lord!" Saren brushed her hand across her skirt. "I am Saren, daughter of Sir Charles Eadwine of Northumberland."

She was silent then, attentive to the father's raised brows. "We found Father Sautrey's name on a book in London, and we believe that book is why William's father is imprisoned." The silence and uncertainty propelled Saren to speak no further of their plight. "I believe I have things of my father's that I must also give to Father Sautrey." Saren watched the priest's face wrinkle in worry and his skin become ashen.

The priest lowered his head before he spoke. "I cannot be of assistance to you. Father Sautrey has been denounced. He is not… I," the clergyman stammered. "I must ask you to leave at once." He turned and hurried away in the same direction he had come, leaving William and Saren to find their way back to the vast entrance.

Their morning's pottage was forgotten, their stomachs growled, and their feet became nagging weights. The duo grew hungry and cranky as the cloaked sun was beginning to set beneath the western hills. As they left the chapel, the friendly nun a few years older than William found them again and whispered in Saren's ear, "Father Sautrey has recanted, though sometimes it is said that he secretively fills in as the priest here at St. Michael's in Coventry." The sister lingered for a long moment, wanting to say more or ask them a question. Still, she shushed them with her finger across her lips and scurried away like a sneaking mouse.

The pair exited the church's iron gate without a word between them. They were onto something; excitement, fear, or both fueled their steps.

Rain wept down upon them as they walked silently; they could not have spoken had they wanted. Instead, they hurried away from the church.

Once away from the church, William glanced around, making sure not to be overheard, and said, "We must find passage home."

"Yes, but first, we must know why Father Sautrey has recanted." Saren's puzzled eyes were longing for rest. "Because he was guilty of heresy," she answered her own foolish question.

They found their own way, as the rains ceased, back toward London without the help of the armed riders. Saren refused to be fooled into paying for unworthy protection. They walked most of the way through the forest in silence, listening to the birds announcing their presence.

William, at last, interrupted the unease and finally asked the question that had been nagging his heart. "Saren, what things do you have of your father's that you wanted to give Father Sautrey today?" He stopped beside the trail, waiting for Saren to answer his question.

Saren turned, hesitant to chat along the trail. She kept walking as she spoke. "Will, I have a book, or several bound books, that my father entrusted me. Secret books to be given to Father Sautrey at St. Othy's in London. He is not there. When I learned he was now in Coventry, I imagined my mission complete." Saren stopped then and turned to William. Taking his hand in hers, she confessed, "I never meant to keep this from you and Ma."

"Well, now you aren't," Will replied. And walked on asking," What is so secret about your family's books?"

"I will show you once we are home, Will. I dread stopping here on the road."

◆　　◆　　◆

Charles grew accustomed to the loneliness, for he preferred the solitude over occupying the war-torn coastline.

Charles wandered, not lost, just a drifting soul searching for his place. He stuck to the paths along the shoreline or high up on the ragged cliffs where he could witness life without him. A presence of this realm now, he could see what Saren and William could not. And his purpose was to keep them safe.

Charles knew that Saren had arrived safely in Coventry with the boy. He was proud of her cunning wit for spotting the lofty thieves who had fooled countless passengers into fearing the woods.

Charles was not surprised when she demanded they trek back to London alone. And just on a second thought, he had dared to follow the youth home through the forest.

There was a chatter of disbelief and shock as they left the cathedral and continued when they left the town's perimeter. Silence followed them as they marched toward the forest. Once there, the forest closed in upon them all. Though only a spirit, Charles feared the omnipresent stillness and darkness that seemed to swallow them from every direction.

They walked on, neither saying a word. Only the heckling of the birds taking flight dared rustle the forest leaves about them. As her father had taught her, Saren watched among the trees for signs of movement.

William, on the contrary, stumbled along with his head hung low.

Saren urged, "Come, Will, we'd best step up and get beyond the forest quickly." She gripped her blade as they hurried their pace.

Suddenly, they heard a low rustling of leaves upon the forest floor, low down to the ground, like the stepping of paws. "It must be a deer or fox," Will suggested. He lowered his head to watch his step, though not appearing too concerned.

"Animals, yes, it could be. But I think that I hear music. Pipes, I hear bone pipes being played." Saren stopped to listen to the unusual noises of the forest around her, her hands on her hips. "It must be from far away, though. The music must be carried upon the wind." They restarted their plodding toward home and beyond the forest.

The travelers were given a lift by a happy trader who had an empty cart after his deliveries to Coventry when he met them en route to London.

Though they were barely armed, *Saren thought her anger would have protected them had they come to harm.* "How could that priest lie to us? Of course, he could have helped us." she fussed.

"He didn't lie to us, Saren. He, too, fears for his life." William's voice bumped as the cart jostled and bounced upon the stones along the road. "We must move on to locate Father Sautrey and pray he arrives back at Jon's cart with a message, as he intended in his letter." William did not ask again about Saren's family's secret book.

They traveled on, too busy hanging to the rickety wagon's rail to continue their discussion. The sun had gone down when they reached London. The lamps were lit as they thanked the cart driver and went home. The streets were crowded with people hurrying home to their families.

Saren grabbed William's arm, stopping him from being trampled at a busy intersection. William jerked his arm from her grip.

"Saren, I'm not a baby. Why do you think I'll walk amidst the horses?" he growled.

Shaking her head, Saren wrinkled her nose. "I wasn't treating you like a baby, William," she protested as she looked up across the street. There stood the mysterious knight who had delivered her and her baby Liam to London, who had also haunted her dreams. He was standing among the crowd, waiting to walk in her direction. She looked away.

The traffic slowed, and William began to trot into the street. Tired from the bouncy passage home, Saren walked behind, not trying to catch up to him. She walked attentively into the street among the other people crossing, not striving to meet, again, the handsome knighted soldier she had met twice before.

But there he was, walking toward her, his smile broad. He held out his hands, this time in greeting. "Good afternoon, My Lady. May I make your acquaintance?" he asked, his smile dazzled by the reflection of the puddles at his feet.

"Good day, My Lord. My name is Saren. Saren Eadwine of Northumberland. And you are?

"Aye, lass. My name is Sir Henry…" he hesitated, recognizing this too-familiar name. Lass Eadwine was a name that he'd repeated over and over. His father, Lord Percy, had repeated the name as his betrothed. And this was she, before him. She had undoubtedly rebuked him and his name. And she, the holder of the key to his future. A smoldering ember deep within his loins grew, as did the opportunity for revenge. His mind flooded with names of the home country. He tried to think of any other name the fair maiden would not recognize. "You may call me Sir Neville if you please," he lied.

They stood hand in hand in the middle of the street as the masses shuffled past without their notice. A man mounted upon a horse at last rode up and hollered, "You best exit the street, or you'll be stomped upon!"

Saren looked about, aghast at the commotion, "I'd best get along. It was nice to meet you, finally." She hurried to the opposite side of the street, where William stood perplexed and scowling.

"Where may I find you again, My Lady?" Sir Henry Percy shouted from the other side.

Saren shouted above the clamor of wheels and feet, "We'll meet again like this one day." She smiled, turned, and hurried to catch up to William.

CHAPTER EIGHT

Betrothed

He knew her name now. And she was who he'd expected her to be. Sir Henry Percy ambled to the corner, his head spinning. He clutched it with his hand. Amid the situation, Sir Percy had failed to cross the street. It was not until he made his way down the street that he looked up to see that he was still on the opposite side of his destination.

Sir Henry Percy walked toward his mother's home once more.

His mother's home was simple and clear of clutter, though not meager in the least. Art of various styles and artists hung tastefully about the walls.

Once she had removed herself from his father's corruption, his mother had made a fine living among the elite who wanted tasteful, unique gowns.

Oil paintings had most recently compensated her for her exquisite ballroom dresses. His mother was a brilliant tailor and employed two young ladies to assist her with the tedious sewing while she crafted her latest fashion piece.

Sir Henry Percy and his mother sat in her parlor when his mother's tailor maids sashayed into the room. Both were past their teen years and obviously on the prowl for marriage, for they repeatedly interrupted Sir Percy and his mother's visit—although it was not much of a visit, for Sir Percy had scarcely spoken a complete sentence.

Irritated by her employees' antics, his mother said, "Son, my dear. Something is troubling you. Am I correct? Let us go out. We can't have much privacy here." She rose while patting his arm and went to fetch her coat.

They had not walked far when he started to speak. His confessions of affection poured from his lips before his mother had asked. "I learned her name but am pressed to turn her over to the Crown," Henry told of his dilemma. However, he failed to mention his father's attempt to betroth her to him for his own selfish gains to obtain secrets that only the girl possessed that the Church desperately wanted to destroy. His parents were not on speaking terms, and this matter would only ignite his mother's wrath toward the man.

He could say no more about the girl, including the yearning she ignited deep in his soul, as he feverishly denied this feeling that interfered with his father's agenda. They walked along in silence, holding hands. He stopped her there along the street as strangers walked past. Looking at her, he could see where tears had streamed down her face. "Why are you crying, Mother? I haven't said anything to make you sad. I've come for your advice."

"My boy, my Henry, I will help you if I can, but I don't know how." They began their walk again along the street, the summer air heavy on their breath. "You've learned her name but not where she lives. You say you brought her and a child here weeks ago on your horse while on duty. And now she's the criminal." His mother recounted the tale as he knew she would set things right in her mind when she jerked Henry to a halt. "She's wanted for heresy. The priest at the court wants her arrested. She must have an English Bible. Come, we must get back to the house. There are things of your father's that it is time you see." They hurried toward her street as she explained, "Your father left letters behind when he joined the royals. I imagine he couldn't be found with them in his possession," she cleared her throat.

His father's wooden chest was locked; his mother had a dreadful time locating the key. "I never imagined there would be a need to open this," she said as she finally unlocked it. "He is a rebel, your father. He plotted and schemed about how to persuade the Crown and, I suppose, the Church. Your father is the undoing of King Richard, for really, he is one of the corruptors of the Church." His mother fell silent then as she riffled through the books and tablets. Lost in her memories, she went quiet for a spell. "The Church does most of the dirty work," she said. "Don't lock that yet, Son. I must find something for you that may help your decision." She came back to where Sir Henry sat.

"Here." She handed him a loose tablet of unbound papers. "These are parts of the New Testament and letters from the Vatican in Rome ordering scripture to read in exhausting the sacrifice of our Lord and diminishing the power of his wisdom, his feminine. And there exists another letter, Henry." She exhaled a deep breath. "A letter from the Abbey at Iona Scotland explains where the Gospel of Mary and other sacred Wisdom is protected, Henry." Henry's mother looked to her son's pondering face. "These ancient books remain missing. Henry's mother sat nearer. "The Church does not want this truth revealed."

Henry took the manuscripts from his mother. "What does Saren have?" he asked.

"The books, or part of them, the books of The Sophia of Jesus Christ," she explained. "The Sophia of Jesus Christ, or maybe The Gospel of Mary, or both. Your troubled heart is what is most worrisome. Do not give her name to the reverend. They will find it. And you don't know where she lives, is that correct? Therefore, you have nothing to lie about."

"What if I see her again?" Sir Percy looked upward to the ceiling. "What do I do when I see her again?" he asked. His smile most enduring.

"Son, when you see her again, follow your heart." His mother rummaged back through his father's letters. "Now, run along," she said, as she had said years ago when he was a boy. "I'll find the letter from the Vatican, at least, for you when you return." She cast her attention to her errant husband's trove. She paused and called to her son, "And don't tell your father of the girl. If she truly is Sir Charles Eadwine's daughter, she holds the greatest treasure that your father has ever sought. And he will stop at nothing to have it."

CHAPTER NINE

Gratitude

Saren and William ambled the London streets again, alert to unusual onlookers. Though Saren had not spoken, William could sense she was looking for someone in particular—*a knight of the king's court, to be exact.*

"You know, Saren, he's not on our side." William shuffled past.

"William, you have no idea what he is," she fumed, rushing toward him. "And why did you mention him, today of all days?"

"Because you are looking for him. I see you. You think that your knight in shining armor will be here to save you," William spat.

"Will, we have serious matters before us. Stop this bickering at once," Saren huffed.

"There you go, sounding like you're my mother again." He walked backward, bumping directly into a guard.

"Ach, lad! Turnabout and walk straight, or you'll be causing a ruckus," scolded the guard.

They arrived at Jon's wheel-less cart to find it ransacked beyond recognition since their last visit. There, beneath the axles, in a closed compartment where the ink and papers had been stashed, Saren placed her note to John Sautrey, requesting his help releasing William's father from Oxford Prison but mentioning nothing of her sacred books.

"We will be lucky to have him come and find this request. I fear this is our last hope to find your pa," Saren confessed. "Come, let's go home and make a plan for when we do hear back, if at all." The duo silently meandered home.

The aroma of good food urged them quickly through the door.

"Roasted chicken from Sir Oldcastle. Their parlor-maid brought it this afternoon. She wished us our best and was sympathetic to your pa's plight," Ma explained.

William clapped his hands. "See here, we are not alone! Then they must know why Pa was arrested returning to London." Nearly jumping with excitement, William broke into a reel: "Ther lordys, erles and barome were slayne…"

The succulent meat sent wafts of moist air from the table. Stewed carrots, singed slightly across the edges, and creamed peas filled each plate. Saren sliced apples to garnish each plate as William continued his merrymaking.

She smiled despite protesting, "Will, you were the one that said we shan't waste our precious time singing."

"Right, Saren. We must eat."

The food was the best any of the trio had tasted in ages. Hardly a word was spoken with their newfound contentment and full bellies. No lamps remained lit that night at the Wynch's home as they all slept peacefully. Saren woke early, intending to read and transcribe more of the Bibles from Jon the mute. As the sun emerged over the horizon, she began instead transcribing and researching the Coptic gift Joseph had given her months ago as they left the Al-Aoura. She hadn't found a pen in William's loot, so she made her own from a piece of kindling from the fire and her ever-sharp knife.

The ink was thick and smooth, like warmed honey. Saren felt comfortable, and she relaxed into her transcribing. Nearing the end of the second page, she found a flow to her writing and precision that she was unaware she possessed.

Each letter, each mark that she drew, became her own unique signature.

Smiling, she was certain the work was intended for the materials she and William had taken from Jon's cart. She studied the issue as she still knew that they were borrowed goods, not stolen. Onward, she worked by the flickering flame and dawn's early glow.

The pages of The Gospel of Mary began to unfold before her as she copied. The numbers, though, were illegible, as she was more uncertain of their meaning and only copied them as they were and carried on. She came to a place in the text and faltered. Saren stuck her makeshift pen back into the bottle of ink, rose from her seat, and went to the shutters, ajar at the one window of the cottage.

She had not spoken of her father for many days and many nights. Looking to the crimson horizon, she spoke to him or of him—she was not sure which, nor did she care. She only knew that he was listening.

The calmness of the morning, like only the quiet before the first light knows the twinkle of the last remaining morning star, could mean nothing less.

Saren prayed to her lost father. She prayed to God. "Dear Father, where art thou? I pray, my dear Lord, my God." She knelt to the ground. "Forgive us, my Lord, for taking the paper and ink from Jon's cart. I know that it was wrong to do. Thank you for delivering us from evils." Saren spoke on with an eager voice. "And thank you, God, for those who prepared our feast… I thank you, my Lord, for my new friends—my new family. For you know, I would have perished by now without their kindness, without your guidance to them, to me, and to this home. I thank you."

Saren looked again toward the last twinkling star and then opened her eyes once more to the Coptic wisdom transcribed where she had left her pages market, with a willow branch, the second of the seven forms of wrath is desire.

'*What is wrath,*' Saren imagined. *Might these wraths be like Christian sins?*

How, then, could one be without desire? Or worse, have no desire? Saren fumbles with the Coptic translation, *or being cynical of others' desires? Too embellished in our material world our day-to-day. Ungrateful and negative, too.*

Saren finished translating many pages as the others in the home stirred. The writing appeared cleaner and clearer toward the end, so she summarized and read her work: "Mary is praised by the Savior because she has not 'wavered'..." Saren called for, Ma.

"Ma, please come and listen to my Coptic translations of The Gospel of Mary. This is the treasure being sought by the Crown and The Church."

Will rose from his bed cranky and hurried out.

Saren worked on relighting a short candle as she spoke, "Remember, 'He who has a mind to understand, let him understand. And He who has ears to hear, let him hear.' And this stanza, 'Blessed are you that you did not waver at the sight of Me. For where the mind is, there is the treasure. the mind that is what sees the vision'. And then it stops."

William bent over, peering at the text, and tried to read it. After little success, he asked, "Saren, could you please teach me to read and to write?" And without waiting for her reply, he added, "I'm off to give my thanks to Sir Oldcastle for the grand meal. Do you have any errands for me, Ma?" he asked.

"No, please share our gratitude as well. That would be fine."

"Yes, Will. I would be delighted to be your teacher. Hurry back," Saren urged.

An Abduction

Sir Henry Percy had arrived late in the evening at his mother's home. The lamps in the cottage remained unlit. Children were no longer scurrying about with their games and chasing in the streets. A summer storm's chill was ripe on the breeze.

He rapped at the door.

When there was no answer, he entered. The house was vacant of all its welcome sparkle. The kitchen's fire was nearly extinguished.

Henry hurried to the kitchen, searching from room to room. The home was vacant.

His father's trunk remained open, spilling its contents across the floor. He could see no sign of his mother.

He laid a log upon the fire and wafted the flame to life. Taking a glowing twig from the flame, Henry walked about the room and lit the candles, returned to his father's trunk, and replaced the contents. As he did so, with his candle nearby, he spotted his mother's rosary heaped upon the floor.

He scooped it into his clutches, and the pounding on the heavy door sent his heart thudding into his throat. Henry rushed from the room to answer the door.

He cautiously cracked the door, looking to see who was paying a visit to his mother's home, as he had been trained to do as a knight. There stood the gray-eyed Father Dudley, who had had him arrested by his peers three days prior. "Excuse me, Father," Henry said, not alarmed at his presence. "May I ask if you have seen my mother this day?" Neither smile nor hospitality touched his lips.

"Why, Sir Percy, you are speaking out of hasty assumptions, are you not? Lad…"

"I am not a lad," Henry interrupted. And by what virtue does a 'hasty assumption' come to mind unless you know of my concerns already?" Henry watched the priest for signs of unease. "Where is my mother, Reverend?" he asked as he watched the priest step from foot to foot upon the hard stone step.

"May I come in, sir?" he asked, his teeth chattering. "We will talk in the house."

"Is my mother safe?" Henry blocked the entrance. "What have you done with her, and why?" he demanded.

"Your mother is fine; she's in the cellar of the Tower of London, waiting for your cooperation to set her free." He spoke with a spattering shiver.

"As you say." Henry stepped aside, allowing the priest into his mother's home, then followed him to the parlor where the fire grew.

There, Father Dudley stood near the mantel and began to state his demands. "I am here, Sir Percy, to make a bargain with you." He gave a labored smile before he went on. "I will give you your mother when you bring your father's forbidden blasphemous letters." He moved away from the fire, then added, "And the girl, Saren Eadwine. I saw you speak to her in the muddy street. She is copying Wycliffe's Bibles like her father, Charles, and distributing them with that boy, as his father has done."

Copying Bibles, yes, this he knew, though nothing of her family's secret book was requested.

Farther Dudley demanded, "I want her arrested immediately. They were seen taking paper and ink from the mute's cart in the city center." He took a greedy gulp of air. "When you meet my requests, I will release your mother." He found his way from the parlor and latched the door behind himself.

Henry swallowed bitterly and went back to his father's chest. No treasures remaining there, only papers and drafts of letters. He packed it all back into the chest, put out the lamps, shut the damper, and went to find his friend, Lord Cobham.

CHAPTER ELEVEN

The Watchtower

William strolled through the crowded streets on his way to the home of his pa's boss, Sir Oldcastle, to thank him for the meal. Sir Oldcastle, known among the elite as Lord Cobham, lived on the good side of town. One did not wander into their welcome arms unless invited. Now, with a perfect explanation for a visit and giddy with energy and stamina from the good night's sleep and the good food, William bounded up the steps of the stone house. There was no gate, and no fence marked the home's perimeter. Only a well-worn stone path led to numerous steps of rock that climbed to an excessively high front porch. With a puzzled demeanor, William shrugged in acceptance. He looked around for a nearby waterline; high tide could be the only explanation for having an entryway raised so high.

He lifted the wrought-iron knocker and let it fall, repeated, then waited.

He heard footsteps, barely loud enough to be a child's, tiptoeing behind the closed door.

William caught the shadow of a tall, slender figure shuffling behind a draped window, and then the door cracked open.

"Good day, Ma'am. I am William Wynch. My father, James, works for Sir Oldcastle. I've come to pass my gratitude to him, Lord Cobham, if I may?" He asked.

The door shut much quicker than it was opened.

Alarmed, William waited. He turned his back to the heavy door and faced the street below. He watched the people going by, the happenings from afar. The vantage point from Sir Oldcastle's home was sublime. He could see the entire town.

The door reopened—this time more easily, as a man of strong build and dark, sun-touched skin opened it. "William, lad Wynch. Please, do come in. What brings you out on this fine morning?"

William entered the great stone house. His worn shoes brushing the polished floor. He stooped to touch the floor's smooth surface and then stood bewildered. "I have never seen wooden floors." William didn't intend Lord Cobham to hear his observation.

Sir Oldcastle turned and gave the lad a subtle nod, saying, "Come, sit. Tell me, how is your mother favoring?"

"She is well, sir—as well as can be expected, Sir." William sat. He gazed upon the tall walls, ornate with artwork and pretty drapes. Each wall held a framed window open to view the scene below. "You have a marvelous home here, high atop the hill, Sir." William's voice trembled.

"Yes, Lad. My home is like a watchtower, and I the watchman. But I don't always like what is to be seen." Sir Oldcastle rose and went to a table in the corner of the room. Wide-eyed in puzzlement, William tried to speak.

"I came to thank you for your kindness." He muffled a nervous choke with the back of his hand.

"Would you care for some water, Lad?" The host fetched a goblet and a pitcher before William could protest. "Here you are, Son, drink this." He handed the cup to William with a steely hand.

"Thank you once more. I came simply to thank you for the elaborate meal you sent last eve." William drank gingerly from the cup of water. "Thank you, also, for the water. You are a generous man."

Sir Oldcastle spoke of the arrest of William's father before William could muster the nerve to approach the issue. "William, Lad. You don't mind if I call you William, do you? I recall your father called you Will."

William nodded.

"Very well. William, as I presume you and your mother are quite aware, your father was completing one of my deliveries when he was arrested." Sir Oldcastle took a sip of his drink before proceeding. "I am doing everything in my power to have him released. As you see"—the gentleman sat down nearer William— "your father is innocent. He has done nothing wrong."

"Aye, Sir. What was he delivering? Your Bibles to London's Osyth's Cathedral, Sir? Bibles?" William asked quickly before thinking of a less harsh way of approaching the issue. The words burst from within.

Sir Oldcastle let out a suppressed sigh, licked his lips, and smiled. "You are a sharp lad. How on earth did you gain this knowledge?"

"It is a long story, really, Sir. But I—we, Will corrected, happened on Jon the Mute's books before he was seized. Pa was, we presumed, delivering like goods."

"What a relief. I was certain poor Jon had them with him when he was arrested. And yes, Jon is… was my transcriber." Sir Oldcastle rose to his feet. "You have the books with you?"

"No, Sir. I do not. My father did, though?"

"Yes. Not original Wycliffe Bibles like those that you now have. But copies that Jon had drawn." Sir Oldcastle walked the floor. The wood creaked beneath his weight at each step.

William watched his feet as if waiting for the floor to break under his heavy build.

"Can you bring me the Wycliffe Bibles, William? I will pay you for your troubles." The man clasped his hands behind his back.

Will stood nearer to the man. "Sir, may I ask, did my father know what the books were? Did he know what he was risking, bringing them from Oxford?"

"Yes, Son. He knew and was learning to read to help spread the word of the Lord.

He believed that the truth must be shared."

William turned and walked across the room to stand before a great window. "He is not innocent, then, in the eyes of the Crown. He is guilty as charged." William turned back to the man, saying, "I would like to… to know what we are fighting for. I must hear the books read, Sir. Read in English." He returned to his seat. "My friend Saren is working to transcribe a Coptic Bible. Her writing is slow— she is getting better, but it would help if we, if I, could hear the Wycliffe Bibles read once."

"Splendid! I would be honored to read from such text. But there comes great risk in being involved with works opposed by the Crown and the Church." Taking an exaggerated breath, Sir Oldcastle asked, "Are you sure you want to take these risks like your father?"

Any tension between the men simmered into vapors as they sat in silence. "We must read these books in their entirety, of course. Then we will continue Pa's efforts," William scooted to the edge of his seat.

"I am working to have his release expedited. I do have friends that may aid him. We need only keep him in our prayers."

"That we can do, Sir. Would you accompany me home? My ma and Saren would welcome your company."

"I shall fetch my cap."

The men navigated the slender steps from Sir Oldcastle's watchtower and headed to Will's cottage.

⬦   ⬦   ⬦

"Hello, the house!" Will bellowed through the door. "I'm back, and I brought a guest for a visit."

Ma bustled from the bedroom chambers. "Oh my, dear boy, I was not expecting company. Dear me." She fluttered about, tidying linens and loose garments.

"No, no, Ma'am. Please do not fret for an instant about my being here. Take heed." Sir Oldcastle kindly grasped her shoulders and held her still. "Good day, Ma'am," he reiterated, giving Ma a slight dip of his head. "I am Sir Oldcastle, my lady. Lord Cobham to some. It is my great pleasure to make your acquaintance."

"S-s-sir Oldcastle!" Ma stammered. "Welcome, then. Please, come sit." Ma pulled a chair out from the table and fetched some ale.

"Where has Saren gone, Ma?" William demanded. "She shouldn't be about all alone!" He careened from the opened shutter.

"She'll be fine, Will. She has taken measures to be careful. I'm afraid we just can't keep that bird in a cage." Ma chuckled as she toweled a goblet with a piece of linen for the unexpected visitor. "I've come to give my condolences, Lady Wynch, and to give my word that I am doing everything feasible to expedite your husband's release." Sir Oldcastle cleared his throat. "We have apparently a leak, a traitor, a spy working among us who tipped someone off about our connections here in the city. The authorities, however, are connecting our every involvement." Sir Oldcastle leaned back while Ma poured the ale.

"William don't feel forsaken by my keeping information from you earlier. I simply wanted your mother's approval of your involvement in these affairs. You see, my boy," Sir Oldcastle explained.

Ma finished pouring the ale. She took a sip and sat before she asked, "Sir, don't mind my assumptions; however, how on earth may you help my husband without alerting the Crown to your own involvement?"

"You are quite correct in your thinking, Ma'am. You see, I was under the impression that Jon the Mute still possessed my Wycliffe Bible when he was captured. Had he that book, we all would have been found guilty. Jon may have been mute, but he certainly was quick-witted." Rubbing his palms upon his trousers, the large man continued. "The Bibles your husband had were unmarked in sealed packages. He did not know what was inside. He was trained to cooperate with the knights and not provoke suspicions." He sipped his ale from the goblet, his great hand agile like a painter's.

"You mean, Sir, he played ignorant about the contents of his deliveries?"

"Precisely, Lad. You are catching on." Sir Oldcastle clapped his hands in appreciation just as Saren burst through the door, sending the room into mayhem.

Her entrance startled everyone except Ma, for she looked nothing like the Saren that had once run through the streets with William. Now, she wore his slacks, heavy loafers, and a work blouse of Ma's, covered by an old work vest that William's pa had worn the summers prior. One of Will's old caps sat upon her mop of curly, short, blunt-cut, boyish hair. Her wide smile was the only part of her face that remained feminine. "Good day. Excuse my rude entrance." Saren, surprised, hid her rosy cheeks.

"Saren, what have you done to yourself?" William asked as he rushed forth. Grabbing her small hand, he pulled her around. "What did you do to your hair, Girl?" he reached to touch her short curls that bobbed beneath the hat's brim. Touching one short curl, her long ebony locks were gone.

"Will, it was nothing. This is best. Now, I do not have to hide my hair. I can go about and do errands for Ma. Find work, even."

"No! You will not," Will barked, surprising himself more than the others in the room. "I mean to say…" He wiped his chin with the back of his hand. "I mean to say, I think we have plenty for you to do here with transcribing the Bibles. That is all." William was now the one who blushed. He sat back at the table to carry on their discussion of plans to work with Sir Oldcastle. William listened as Ma introduced the gentleman to Saren. He listened to their needless chatter, but he could not take his eyes from her curls beneath his old cap or her shapely breasts beneath his pa's old vest. He didn't trust his eyes to conceal his feelings.

◆   ◆   ◆

"Saren, shall we read of the Book of Mark? You are comfortable with Matthew. This work of yours is grand." Sir Oldcastle turned each page Saren had copied with grace.

"Yes, Sir. Please may we… please?" Saren moved silently about the table, seemingly unaware of William's transfixed eyes that followed her.

Sir Oldcastle read then by candlelight. Saren followed his reading from over his shoulder, pausing him only where her writing became less clear.

Sir Oldcastle took breaks only for ale and once for his own relief. Otherwise, he read uninterrupted into the night. Those who listened never slowed him with their questions or further comments. Not until he read the final verse did Saren relax. She stood now behind William, her hands resting on his shoulders. She asked, "Sir Oldcastle, where do we distribute the books? Not many people can read these. The masses, the people, don't read. The elite do, the Crown." Saren stammered a moment. Faltering in her thought, she sat.

"That is a grand question, Saren. And one that is of grave concern." Sir Oldcastle looked upon the listening faces and said, "The upper class, those who are educated— their numbers are growing. We must seek these people. This group must be shown the truth to empower all." He scratched his brow. "This re-culturing of a society takes time." Sir Oldcastle sipped his ale and gently returned his cup to the table. Rising to his feet, he went to William's chair and stood, resting his hand on the lad's shoulder. He added, "I have just had a thought, an idea, or I would have asked William this beforehand, but there is no time to ask him privately. William," Sir Oldcastle knelt before him. "If I appoint you, would you be willing to devote your life to the Lord? Mrs. Wynch, Saren, William, would you be interested in accepting my appointment for William to attend seminary at Oxford, at Balliol College?"

The room fell silent as everyone exchanged uncertain glances.

Ma, who had remained standing, walked about, her hands at her hips. She nodded, then said in a wavering voice, "How will we ever pay for our boy to attend Oxford, Sir?" She went back to take her place at the table.

"This is my offer to you, your son, and your family, Mrs. Wynch. William has the proper heart and mindset. Now, he only requires education to become a priest among the nobility and to lead them from their debauchery." Sir Oldcastle sat back at the table before continuing. "Within the walls of the Church, William would be our greatest asset."

"William would be a Poor Priest, as my father was?" Saren erupted.

"No, Saren. Not a 'Poor Priest,' an Oxford clergyman of the Church." Sir Oldcastle brushed his whiskers with his hand. "William, you could then plant the seeds of truth wherever you could without risking yourself." Sir Oldcastle looked between the two young people before he caught a breath of air and bit his lower lip. "It is your choice, of course. For there would be sacrifices of your own to contend with." Both men at the table blushed. "I never presumed …" Sir Oldcastle stopped mid-sentence.

"No, there is nothing to presume, Sir. We are good friends, best friends, Sir. That is all." William repressed his heart as he looked across the table to Saren.

"We must plant the seed to reform the Church, My Lad. Or we shall never be freed of bondage." Sir Oldcastle paced the dirt floor, looking to William, then to his mother, then to Saren. He said, "Those endeavors take time to nurture, to spread. The people of the Church have been repressed for countless generations. They love the Church, its familiarity, and the routines. Latin is their comfort. Is it not comforting to return to Mass each Sunday as you have since you were a girl and have the same experience? Comfort is found in the familiar, even when the familiar is unclear, no doubt."

Ma rose from the table and stood behind Will's chair as if preventing him from leaving the room, "Sir Oldcastle. We have not been able to attend Mass for years. We haven't enough for penance each week." She smiled, saying, "When we did attend regular Mass, I did find it comforting, the routine of it." Ma squeezed Will's shoulders, reached for the kettle, and returned it to the flame.

Sir Oldcastle nodded despite the misalignment, cleared his throat, and added, "I only imply that there shall be many citizens who do not wish to see the Church changed. Though it will continue to cost them dearly, they won't want familiarity taken from them."

Will stood and paced near the door. "Sir, it is not the sacrament, the Eucharist, that must change. The power, the hand that controls the Church, must change." Will fetched the warmed pot and poured hot tea for everyone around the table. "My reading and writing are meager, my Latin a disaster, Sir Oldcastle." He spooned his broth. "How will I manage?"

"Yes, my boy. This magnitude of change can only begin internally, from within the Church herself," Sir Oldcastle sipped from his cup. "You've your work cut out for you; I imagine. And I can help."

"Yes, I will do anything. Anything that I am called to do." William smiled at Saren as she stood.

"Is it possible, Sir Oldcastle, to have William placed within the Church? To teach the masses from the inside?" Saren returned to stand behind William. He craned his neck to see her movements without shifting away from her touch. "If we learn from what is happening now, it seems that the Church and the Crown punish those who tell the truth." She sighed in disgust. "Look what has happened with Father Sautrey and Jon. The crowd turned on them. We will not make those same mistakes. We mustn't continue the same way to make change. We will distribute our copied Bibles to the people of stature, like yourself, Sir Oldcastle."

♦ ♦ ♦

The night was heavy over him. William lay motionless, the beating of his heart the only interruption to sleep.

Sleep that never arrived, no matter how still he rested nor how eagerly he wanted it. He could not slip from consciousness.

When he imagined leaving for training, his hands grew sweaty, clammy, and wet. The mental challenges did not worry him. It would be a pleasure, even fun perhaps, to test his thoughts. Leaving Ma was not the trouble that found him. They were always close and would always be. His father crossed his mind, sleeping in prison. *Was there a bed for him, or did he sleep upon the cold, hard floor?* He pondered.

He had to do something, somehow. This life of oppression was ceaseless. Though he had never known anything else, there were freedoms and treasures of this life to which he and all others were entitled.

William decided then that he would go gladly. If they would take him?

But she crossed his mind. Walking about in his old trousers with her hair cut short like a boy's. The short hair made her look so different. So much less like… like a girl. The short hair gave her the aura of a woman.

William rolled to his side, trying to lose the thoughts of Saren.

Instead, he felt the heat of his flesh beneath the blankets. He rolled back to stare at the dark wall. He closed his eyes only to remember Saren's touch upon his shoulders. His body quivered at the thought of her hands upon him. Everywhere.

William woke after dawn. Routine noises from the kitchen broke his deep sleep. He stirred, his body limp and exhausted from only a few hours of sleep. He sat to discover his linens were soaked from his dreams of the night.

He lay back, gathering his wits about him.

Their friendship had evolved into something more, something beyond a brother-sister bond.

They were growing older and wiser to nature's ways, but neither had considered, much less spoken of, a future together.

William lay staring up at the ceiling rafters illuminated in the morning light. He grumbled to himself, *"It has taken the suggestion of marriage being forbidden for a man to yearn for a woman."* Shaking his head at his logic, he rose. "And she has her sights elsewhere," he groused.

Being the last to have his pottage, William was less chatty and made himself scarce, hurrying off on a less-than-urgent errand.

William left the following week with Sir Oldcastle for Oxford. Chatty and giddy though he was, he hated leaving his home and his ma.

They sat together, weeping. Saren reassured them with her words: "This is a step forward for all for us. A large step. Ma and I have each other to lean on." She avoided looking at William directly for fear she might cry. "We will always be here as your family. No matter what." She stood and went to hug William around the neck.

She then gave William her latest copy of Wycliffe's Bible. "I left all names and dates upon the pages. You must keep this hidden."

"I shall," Will said, wrapping the forbidden bible in a woolen scarf. And study my Latin," he burst, his voice cracking. My, it has been so long since I studied anything." He shook his head. Saren, I will miss you," he said as he squeezed her hand and left.

CHAPTER TWELVE

A Mutual Acquaintance

Sir Henry Percy stood no chance of locating the letters that his father had once kept, nor did he know the whereabouts of the girl. They had only met thrice before. He needed to speak to someone who might know of his father's affiliations opposing the Church, and the one that may know was his father's friend and his wife, who was a client of Henry's mother. He took a carriage early the next morning for the mansion on the hill, overlooking the city ablaze with early morning light. He climbed the countless steps to reach Lord Cobham's front door.

He hadn't a chance to knock as the door was hurled open to welcome him in for ale and cakes. Lady Cobham had watched him arrive and was disappointed when his mother was not with him, but she welcomed him in just the same. She then left to fetch her husband for his early morning visitor.

Sir Percy dared not mention the abduction of his mother, the dressmaker, to one of her paramount clients for fear of tarnishing her business. He waited impatiently in the parlor.

He heard their voices whispering down the hall long before they arrived together, "No, dear. I did not send for Sir Percy's salutations so early this day. I will send your regards to his mother. Thank you, My Love." Sir Oldcastle, or Lord Cobham as the higher class knew him, deposited a kiss on his wife's small hand.

"Welcome to our home, Sir Percy. What brings you forth at such an early hour?" He walked toward Sir Percy with his hand offered.

"Please forgive my intrusion, My Lord." Henry shook his hand. "My mother has been kidnapped, Sir. I didn't know who else would help," he announced in one breath. For, Lord Cobham was the diplomat of all civil affairs of the region and to all the people, wealthy and poor.

"Why did you not go to the knights' council, Sir Percy? You are a knight. Could you not have taken this to the court?" Lord Cobham held his breath, then answered his own question, "Unless the matter involves your father's affairs?"

"Yes, my lord. Reverend Dudley came to the house not long after I had arrived and demanded that I exchange my father's letters for my mother. He has her prisoner in the cellar of London's tower." Henry walked about the room, rubbing his palms together as he spoke.

"The cellar at London's tower? Why that is preposterous. We must go for her immediately," Lord Cobham demanded. "There is more, sir." Henry stepped forward, nearly whispering. "I'm to find a young girl that he saw stealing books from Jon the Mute's wagon a few weeks past.

He accuses her of heresy and declares that I know her whereabouts." Henry turned and gazed out the window.

"Where are you to find this girl, Henry? May I call you Henry?"

"Yes, sir. You have known me since I was but a lad. Before that, I presume." Sir Percy turned to share his concerned smile.

"Yes, we must have your mother released at once." Lord Cobham turned to leave the room but hesitated before the door. "Sir, what does this girl look like? You have seen her, have you not?"

"Yes, Lord Cobham, I do know what she looks like. I have seen her. Three times, I have seen her here in London." Sir Percy took hesitant steps about the room before he replied. "Sir, I escorted her here the day prior to King Henry's coronation. There was strife on the outskirts of London. We were summoned, my regiment, to the front." He closed his eyes as he retold the day that had changed his heart. "I was ordered by Lord Beauchamp to bring the poor lass and her infant to the city where they would be safe."

"I see." Deep in thought, Lord Cobham placed his hands into his pockets. "Why did Lord Beauchamp select you, Sir, to escort her into the city?"

"I do not know, Sir. I was not at liberty to ask. However, I reckon, and reckoned then, that he called upon me because I had the swiftest horse." Though he knew then, as all his fellow knights knew, it was because Henry's father had ordered Beauchamp to protect his only son and give him the safest orders.

"Yes, presumably so. Where did you take the girl?"

"Lord, I left her at the outskirts of the city with the password to open the gates, then rode back to the front lines."

"And the second time you saw her, Henry? Where was this? And when?"

"I bumped into her in the street at the market square. I was on duty, making my late rounds, when I was startled by music or piping nearby. We all were, there near the city center. A large lad danced a jig backward and into me, and I was pushed into the girl, knocking her backward into the mud."

"And this was where Father Dudley saw you speaking to her?"

"Yes, but I didn't catch her name then, either. I would not have recognized her as the girl that I had brought into the city had her hat not been knocked off, spilling her bounty of coal-black curls. She quickly stuffed her mane back into the cap just before I spoke to her. I told her not to hide it. Then we parted ways. Father Dudley was watching her and the boy she was with. He said that they took something from the mute's cart there in the square."

Lord Cobham bit his lip. "Henry, she is the woman with the baby the guardsmen searched for after Jon the Mute's arrest that day?" He shook his head at the coincidence. "The Crown seized the mute and had him executed, but never were able to find proof of his charges. She is presumed to hold the proof of Jon the Mute's guilt."

"The girl had a child in her arms. It could be the same girl. Not many young girls walk about with such hair, a baby, and no scarf on their heads."

"No, and I don't believe this girl knew she was getting books when she spoke to Jon the Mute. I believe she thought that she was getting food." Lord Cobham went to fetch his overcoat. "Come, my son. I know where she is. And I know who she is, and she's as innocent as your mother."

Sir Percy had discovered a goldmine of information here during this brief visit, and for now, he was certain of the face of his betrothed. And what a beautiful face she has, he thought, grinning. And would not his father, Lord Percy of Northumberland, be overjoyed? She also possessed what he desperately sought, nearly as much as the dreadful Father Dudley. Henry's challenge was now to keep his heart like stone, his mother safe and his true name from falling on Saren's ears, though, he imagined, *being her betrothed must work to my advantage.*

CHAPTER THIRTEEN

A Barter

Saren could not speak; her mouth was dry, and her fingers trembled. She found comfort in making herself busy among this unexpected company and bustled about the kitchen, looking for small chores that needed tending.

Ma put a stop to her unease. "Come, Saren. We have guests. Please come sit among us," she demanded. She returned to Sir Oldcastle's Lord Cobham as she had grown to know him and his young friend, Sir Percy's, conversation. Saren reluctantly went and sat near Sir Oldcastle and filled her teacup. Sir Neville was, in truth, Lord Percy's son. He had not given her his true identity days ago on the street when she had told him her name, and now he was having Sir Oldcastle ask for her help in finding his mother's release? He must also be seeking her father's sacred books. Their betrothal had not been mentioned. And *I won't dare be the one to do so,* she thought.

Though she had not joined the conversation, she had been listening. "I will go for your mother's freedom," she said. Saren drank from her cup, sighed deeply, and continued, interrupting Sir Oldcastle, "He has no proof of me having done wrong; I know what he is looking for. Moreover, I know what Reverend Dudley fears. He only needs to hear the words come from his own lips."

"Saren, you can't do this. We need you here to complete the transcriptions." Ma began to weep.

Saren went to her and knelt, taking Ma's hand. "Ma, I'm not afraid of this priest. He must listen and hear the truth if he is truly a man of God." Saren's knees shook, and she stood, imagining that if *I agreed to this and left, maybe Sir Percy would have the cottage searched. Or, perhaps, he knows that my freedom will ensure that I will lead him to his treasure?*

Sir Percy stood with his hands in front of him as if speaking to a higher-ranked officer. "Saren, Ma Wynch, this priest is not a man of God. He is a man of the cloth and will do anything to protect his wealthy stature in the Church." Sir Percy looked at the faces in the room before he went on. "He is a wolf among us—the devil in disguise—and ought not to be trusted." He accurately described his own presence there among them.

Everyone began speaking at once; urgency left them anxious to bring Sir Percy's mother home. Ma clapped her small hands together. "We must remain focused here, together. We cannot risk being consumed by the wickedness of the situation. Now, please, everyone, keep yer wits." Ma rose and began preparing food. There was not much to prepare, but she cooked what she had for her guests: boiled potatoes, sausage, and two eggs. They ate in silence, unwilling to share their plans, ideas, or solutions.

The conversation began again about Sir Percy's father's missing letters from the ancient Abby in Iona as Saren helped Ma Wynch clear the table. She hoped that Sir Percy was sincere as she spoke. "What would be different in your father's letters? Why would Father Dudley not be just as happy to have our Wycliffe translations?" she asked as she returned to the table.

"That is a good question, Saren. Please fetch your books for us to examine," Sir Oldcastle requested.

Saren pondered a breath before getting her things when Henry's eyes locked on hers.

He explained, "My father holds proof in those letters from the monks at Iona that the Gospel of Mary exists. Not the Gospel itself..." his eyes never blinking. "It's whereabouts is now being revealed."

Removing herself silently, Saren held her heart with both hands as if to quiet its drumming. *Ma and I are in grave danger here*; she knew and retrieved the sacred book, tucked it safely inside her vest she'd worn of Pa Wynch's, and grabbed her latest transcriptions.

"Whatever became of the babe?" She heard Sir Oldcastle's question. "I was under the impression that the Crown was searching for a girl with a wee infant?" he added.

"The wee lad suffered long enough, sir," Ma explained. "Saren rescued 'em from a ransacked village while on her pilgrimage here."

Knowing that Father Dudley sought simple proof to condemn his father, Lord Percy and that his father held that proof in his own possession, the need to obtain the secret treasures that Saren held for himself grew. Sir Percy held his position quietly and did not hear the conversation in its entirety. He was consumed with his scheme of gaining her secret trove for himself, precisely as Father Dudley schemed. He stood in thought near the kitchen flame as Saren returned to the table with her satchel.

Raising the heavy satchel to the table, she asked, "Sir Percy, have you ever heard of your father's involvement?"

He ambled nearer, brushing his trousers. "No, I have never heard of any of this before now," he lied, "Mother started to show me what was in his chest. But… she was distracted," he confessed, thinking of his own dilemma that he had taken to his mother and how trivial that dilemma truly was. "She had left it open, left the lock off, saying how she'd get back to it later. We went for a walk and later returned to her parlor. That was the last time that I saw her."

Sir Percy watched Saren momentarily and then asked her frankly, "What did you and William remove from the mute's cart in the square the day Father Dudley saw you?"

"We took paper and the ink I'm using for transcribing." She held the vat of ink high. "That is all."

"Very well, we will take what you have left of the supplies to Father Dudley, along with your story of innocence. But what of your father's letters? Lord Cobham asked.

"I know nothing about them; all that remains in his chest are loose notes, nothing of any value to a minister or any other pawn of the Church."

"William and I did place a note for Father Sautrey beneath Jon's cart, hoping to find his father's release. We must return immediately and see if any response has been left for us," Saren whispered to Sir Oldcastle, though knowing no response was there, as she had checked earlier herself and the letter remained.

At that, Sir Oldcastle spoke up. "Come, Sir Percy. We shall search for this note and fetch your mother at once. Saren, you, my girl, will not be used in this exchange, but thank you for your willingness." Sir Oldcastle squeezed her hand. "Instead, may I take your paper and ink as evidence of what was taken? Of course, I will replace it." The men gathered their wraps and Saren's loot, thanked Ma for the meal, and left, with not two words exchanged between Sir Percy and Saren.

Saren went about her evening duties, consumed by her bitter thoughts of Sir Percy's father, Lord Percy's role in this charade. And of her own father not returning home and how the repressed English Bibles were only a cover to a magnificent lie. For much grander truths were being repressed, Saren knew. Truths that her father had never known.

Sir Percy's mother was released in exchange for the feeble amount of paper and ink that Saren and William had pilfered from the mute's cart. It seemed a small penance for his mother's life; Sir Percy was horrified by the evil father's wickedness. He had told the priest, "I did not find the girl. But I found the boy, who knew nothing of her whereabouts, and he gave me back what they had stolen and begged to be forgiven of charges."

Sir Percy watched the criminal, Father Dudley, trying desperately to find the ransom unjust. He could not and released his mother to him, saying, "Sir Henry Percy, you are a wise, young lord and ought to know exactly what I am seeking. You know as well as I that your father, Lord Percy, is here in London looking for the lass, Saren, and her sacred book. Why do you protect her from your own father, boy? For your own benefit, of course. And which is why I release your mother to you, Sir. You are now my servant for the cause."

Henry dared not look down at Father Dudley's gray eyes. He swallowed hard, hoping the evil man would never learn of his betrothal request to the girl. Perhaps this alone was somehow his path of vengeance.

Taking his mother's strong arm in his own, they strode away from the Tower of London.

Father Dudley returned to his intricate office overlooking the courtyard of Temple Church. He began to draft a letter detailing his newfound knowledge and suspicions of Lord Percy's son working for his own benefit and against his father's agenda.

They arrived late in the day at his mother's home. The house was cold as a tomb and dank and smelled of stale mead. "Argh, my lasses have not been nearby. Why could they not keep the house warm and clean while I was away? They most likely stole from me and pillaged my belongings during my leave," Henry's mother fumed.

"Mother, dear. Take heed. You have been through a great ordeal. Now, settle yourself at home. I will set the fire and make some broth. You go and tidy up," Sir Percy commanded.

His mother grumbled as she walked from the room but stopped near the doorway and asked, "You found the girl, then. What did she have that the reverend wanted so badly?"

"Yes, Mother. I found the girl. But she had nothing that Father Dudley didn't already have. She was falsely accused," he lied, the words sticking to the roof of his mouth like clay as he realized Saren's motive in offering to come in his mother's exchange. He now understood that Saren realized her value was in leading him to her trove.

CHAPTER FOURTEEN

The Arrest

Saren had but one delivery that morning. She gathered her satchel and hurried about her business. The town was excessively silent; the usual businessmen and ferries were nowhere to be seen. Uneasiness hung upon the morn, not unlike the calm before a storm. At Ma's request, Saren hurried beyond town, toward Sir Oldcastle's house on the hilltop, to leave her collection of Proverbs, and another Wycliffe Bible that Jon the mute had given her moments before his execution.

She walked; her head dropped low as if trying to shield herself from the storm she could not yet see. Saren rounded the hill toward Oldcastle's great house to see a dozen or more horses and riders approaching, surrounding the home before her.

Saren stopped there in the open, aghast. Frozen in her doom, she watched. One rider took heed and motioned to her.

In one breath, she spun on her heels and raced down the path. Dodging and diving, she ran on. She tripped once over her shoes, which were much too large.

Saren slipped down a side street near town and hid behind a splintered fence. She kneeled close to the ground and decided she'd best stash her forbidden books. A rider rode past, then another. Saren sat motionless. She had to move quickly, for they would see her in plain sight on their return.

Scanning the view from the road, Saren decided the bank along the Thames was the best hiding spot to stash her satchel of transcribed English Bibles before she hurried home to warn Ma Wynch.

A gust of wind blew up from the sea as Saren neared the rocky riverbed. The first outcropping she came upon was perfect—too perfect and the most obvious of hiding places. She hurried past. A mangled bush protruded from the moss-covered rocks rooted in peat, dry and spongy. She pulled it free and placed her satchel and cap snug beneath, pressing a large stone to secure the moss from the shifting stones.

Despite the chill breeze gaining gusto, Saren removed her coat and carried it slung over her shoulder. Slowly, she maneuvered her way to the slums to not draw attention to herself.

As she slipped into the house, she began to tremble. Ma sat her down and poured her broth. Saren began to weep. "Ma, they are arresting Sir Oldcastle. The mounted guards were there. One saw me before I ran. I hid my satchel of Bibles and cap near the river. I think we best leave here. Would Sir Oldcastle lead them to us, somehow?" Saren dried her tears. Sir Percy entered the home without knocking. Without waiting for any welcome, he gave his own account of the arrest of Lord Cobham. His story wavering only slightly from his unique vantage point. Saren willingly told Sir Percy where she had hidden her satchel of Bibles, but they both agreed to leave it lying for the time being. Ma interrupted the conversation, demanding, "Leave the books away for a spell. Give time for this all to pass. Then we can begin again."

Sir Percy sat suddenly on the settle near the kitchen's open flame. "I retrieved a note left at Jon's cart by Father Sautrey. He resides at St. Osyth's here in London," he smiled.

Saren missed her work copying the Bible, her hands now idle after nearly one week of continual writing. She decided to focus her efforts on her family's sacred book instead, as time and her now meager supplies aloud.

The path along the water's edge was heavily trodden. More so than Saren had recalled from the week prior. Cold rain began to prick at her hatless head. For a moment, Saren smiled at retrieving her cap as much as her father's leather satchel from beneath the mossy sanctuary. On she walked into the day to locate her hidden trove.

Traveling in the opposite direction and not having been down this path in days, the scenery appeared suddenly unfamiliar. On Saren pressed, humming one of her father's gentle tunes. The worn trail began an abrupt decline that she did not recall. Had she overlooked her stash?

Turning with an anxious stride, she retraced her steps. The scenery became more familiar. Her rejected, obvious hiding spot had been ransacked. Gleeful that she had not chosen the obvious hiding place, she trudged forward and stepped beyond. However, upon reaching her stone covering, she realized it had been loosened and her father's leather satchel removed.

Sir Percy stashed Saren's satchel before the door and burst into the Wynch cottage with the wind.

His face cracked into a smile despite the chill. "Sir Oldcastle has been sentenced to death for his crimes of heresy," Henry said, knowing well that Father Dudley had had a hand in Sir Oldcastle's swift arrest.

Talk erupted incessantly between Sir Percy and Ma Wynch. Saren rushed forward, grabbing the table to steady her balance.

Sir Percy interrupted a second time and announced with a stammering voice, "Sir Oldcastle shall be executed by fire."

Saren felt a trembling in her soul, for this knight's words had no sorrow to be heard.

At that moment, as he began to tell of the abduction of her precious books, she realized Sir Percy was the only other whom she had entrusted with her secret moss-covered stone hiding place. She kept this secret to herself.

Saren studied the Coptic letters of The Gospel of Mary well into the night. The candle burned to a puddle, yet she continued her translations. She found five names other than Wycliffe's within the last remaining book of Jon the Mute's. All but one she recognized as having stepped down from the Lollard society, according to Sir Oldcastle. The last name, John Sautrey, Wycliffe's assistant, had once been arrested and served as the attending priest at Saint Osyth's. She sought to locate the other translators. They had all recanted long before and had done so to avoid arrest.

"The Crown is not as powerful as the Church to amend righteousness. Why, then, am I?" Saren asked herself.

"I can, though, warn Father Sautrey with my next letter. *And this letter shall be kept a secret,*" she thought.

The sky remained clear, empty like a blank canvas. People gathered in the city center, wearing the smiles that people have when seeing friends after a long absence. On this clean, clear day, they were happy for the opportunity to dress in their best, wash and tidy their skinny children, and go out. It was a social event, the excitement bustling from the center. The conversation of commoners, of the simple folk who were uneducated to the truth, was heard.

This naivete was not their own fault, their own doing, yet no one had taken a stand for change, done otherwise to avoid confrontation, and done nothing to ensure that their children and grandchildren would do better.

They knew why they had come. Barbaric acts oft do not appear that way when carried out by those in power. The actions of those with power overshadow those of the common man. When the simple man resists, his voice is seldom audible; it is irrelevant to execute a commoner because no one beneath him feels the effect. The example is then made of a prestigious man.

By law, citizens were required to attend an execution. Yet, they also appeared out of their underlying need, an unconscious need, or a morbid fascination whereby they may gain a sense of righteousness that justice is being done against the sins for which they themselves could never be redeemed. The lynching post was erected atop smooth stone supporting the blackened pole—a pole that survived the heat of the last flame. Sir Oldcastle's shirt was torn loose about the lapel, his feet bare, hands bound snug behind his back. No hat rested upon his graying mop of hair; an abundance of heavy whiskers covered his once-smooth face.

Saren had never seen Sir Oldcastle without his finery and would not have recognized him in a crowd. She had hated to come out this day, but Ma reasoned there would be suspicions had they not. And that was most certain, for guards were walking among the crowds, scribbling in tablets.

A slender soldier passed near and nodded to Sir Percy. "Good day, Sir. Is your mother not well this fine day?" he asked, looking inquisitively at Saren's striking features.

She did not notice.

"Aye, sir. She is not," he lied.

"Very well. And good day, my…" He hesitated. "Lad." The uniformed guard bobbed his head to Saren, never taking his eyes from her loose curls.

The sun's warmth intensified as kindling was carried in by guards. Books arrived in boxes and crates. Saren could not help but cover her mouth when she recognized a few of her works. Though neither her name nor mark was in the books, they bore her script.

Numerous copies of Wycliffe's Bibles were stacked at the black post's base.

Sir Percy tugged at her sleeve. She dropped her hands from her face to see the same armed guard watching her. Saren quickly looked at him and smiled. Alas, all she could do was smile a forced smile though tears streamed down her face.

Sir Oldcastle was escorted up the stone mound. His bare feet slipped upon the rock before he was tied to the burnt post.

A bald man dressed in knightly clothes read Sir Oldcastle's title and the accusations against him. He spoke of Oldcastle's heresy, then asked, "Do you, Lord Cobham, Sir Oldcastle, have any final words?"

Sir Oldcastle looked around the crowded street. Tears fell from his dark eyes as he stammered, his head stooped. As he raised his head, he spoke loudly and clearly. "Awake to righteousness and sin not: for some have not the knowledge of God: I speak this to your shame."

Their friend recited words from the First Corinthians. Saren knew these words and looked up; her face puffy from crying. Saren was the only witness who wept as Sir Oldcastle spoke.

"Awake to righteousness, and sin not," Sir Oldcastle echoed.

Saren caught her breath in fear that someone would gag him. He was quiet then as they brought torches around.

Sir Oldcastle continued as the smoke rolled. "Now this I say, brethren, that flesh and blood cannot inherit the Kingdom of God."

The flames licked upward, covering his trousers, his shirt, and his hair. His words continued. "Death is swallowed up in Victory." Sir Oldcastle fell silent, motionless, as the flame consumed him until the anguish of death encompassed the silence.

The smoke rose, spilling into the sky like Saren's ink bottle across an empty page. She slipped away from Sir Percy, away from the masses of jeering onlookers and Sir Oldcastle's last belts of pain. Ducking behind the nearest brick corner, Saren lost herself. Once out of sight, her stomach clamped. She swallowed and swallowed harder, but the venomous bile surfaced in her throat. She wrenched forward, emptying herself of all the contents of her soul, until her body looked as if it had lost everything. She shivered uncontrollably for several moments. Regaining her composure once there was nothing more to empty, but her breath, Saren ran. She ran away from the hollering and shouting of the people. "They know not what they say," she said. "They know not what they do." Saren ran from the smoke, the smell of smoldering flesh, the cheering crowd, and the fight within her heart that was never to be won. Saren ran.

CHAPTER FIFTEEN

Truth Prevails

Charles manipulated his pipes with the wind of the earthly realm to sing at his command. He knew he could orchestrate such harmony as a shield against evil.

This power he maintained with the humility that he had harnessed in grace. Sitting near Saren as she slept, Charles hummed a gentle tone to fill her sleep and shield her from the many evils that sought her.

He knew the sacred book rested securely beneath her bed of straw. He knew this family's curse that she inherited must be removed or destroyed before she was killed. Charles, unable to manipulate the physical realm of the earthly world, loathed this predicament. He played the bone bagpipes, hoping to spark Saren to act.

He prayed through the drone of his own music.

Hearing Saren begin to stir from sleep, he continued a softer chant. When she rose with a start, he ceased his music and saw her take the sacred book from the straw and place it on the table near her bed.

$$\diamondsuit \qquad \diamondsuit \qquad \diamondsuit$$

Saren had received no response from Father Sautrey—nothing. The priest had been arrested and had vanished like daffodils in late June.

She slept in bursts with peaceful dreams of studying maps with her father on their hard-packed dirt floor back in Northumberland as he played a soft melody on his bagpipes. She awoke from a horrific nightmare filled with peril, dread, and death. It appeared as an inky smoke that filled the skies and woke her with a humming of uncertainty that she could not explain. The night remained cloaked about her, unwilling to step down for even the sun. Frustrated, she rolled to her side and propped herself up. She saw her father's sacred book spread upon her bed table, not where she had secretly placed it. The vague, early morning memory of waking and retrieving it before being fully awake caused her heart to flutter with urgency to secure the book somewhere safe, destroy it, or hide it?

Saren sat, reaching for her blade, and pulled her shawl upon her chilled back. Since there was no flame to be had, she silently slipped from her slumber and to the embers of the cooking fire to attain warmth. Waking Ma in her angst, she hurriedly coaxed the flame to life.

Ma Wynch came in to set the kettle.

"What have I done, Ma?" Saren held her breath. "Sir Percy is after this sacred book of books. It is he who removed the satchel from the moss, and it is he that led the Crown to Sir Oldcastle and now Father Sautrey." Saren began to weep. "If he wants this book, why has he not yet taken it?" Tears began to streak her ivory cheek. "The letters that his father, Lord Percy, possess prove my books' existence, and he knows I have the ancient treasure in my position. Ma, what have I done? It was I that pushed William to leave," Saren sobbed.

"Now, dear?" Ma Wynch hurried about the cooking fire.

"Ma, I've had a vivid dream this morning." Saren was not yet prepared to leave her weapon lie after such frightful dreams, and she clutched her knife tightly. "The sacred books are what the Crown and the Church seek. Also, they are what Lord Percy and his son, Sir Henry, are after. Not the Bibles. Not me." Saren's thoughts churned aloud to Ma Wynch.

Ma repeatedly rubbed her crying eyes. "I think not, girl. I have not slept for a moment. "Ma rubbed her tired eyes again. "Are you certain this is what is sought?"

Turning her back to the warming glow of the young flame, Saren covered her mouth with her hand. "Ma, I took my father's book from beneath my bedding, where I safely stowed it and laid it out early in the morning." Saren remained curious as she described the morning's events. "I am so diligent concealed it, yet I rose before I woke and fetched it. Come, Ma. See for yourself."

Across the smooth wooden surface of the settle, her family's ancient book remained on display.

Ma covered her mouth, though a smile penetrated her lips. She opened to the first page and wiped her mouth across her sleeve.

Saren's voice trembled. "My quest was to see the compiled books to Jon the Mute, but he was murdered. He was to take them to Father Sautrey at St. Othys' Cathedral. We tried that. Then I tried to take them to Sir Oldcastle, and he, too, was murdered. Now, I have not gotten any word from Father Sautrey in weeks. He's now been arrested and has vanished." Saren wiped her tears, stood, and paced the floor as William had taught her to do while she contemplated her next move.

"Then, my child, this is the transcribing to focus upon." Ma raised the leather-bound document. "We shall, at last, know precisely what we have that is so powerful." Ma smiled, patting Saren's hand and setting the book before her. Saren cupped the book tenderly as though the papyrus pages, brittle from the years, would crumble like ancient bones. "We were not to open this book. She paused before telling Ma of her and her father's night upon the Al-Aoura. And of the ship's Egyptian captain, Joseph, and his transcribing through the night. Wiping a tear that filled her eye, she added, "Pa will know where we should take it."

Saren rubbed her head and pressed her temple. The feeling upon her nagged her so that her ears began to ring. She stopped fussing with the document and sat cupping her head. "Ma, would you make us some broth?"

Ma hurried to fetch water without speaking.

The ringing in Saren's ears lessened as she sat cupping her head. With deep breaths and a calming heart, she silently forgave herself for what she perceived as a failure to protect the sacred books.

In her calm demeanor, she could not help but smile as the ringing in her ears ceased, to be replaced for one fleeting moment by the loving drone of her father's pipes in the distance.

Ma sat near with broth for each of them. "Are you well, child?" she asked.

"I am well, Ma. Yes, and thank ye." She cupped her warm tea with both hands. "I know what we do is right." Taking a few sips from her cup, she rested it beyond her reach to avoid any potential spills. The candle's glow revealing the ancient red seals placed there centuries before.

"What does this mean?" Ma pleaded, pointing at the seal.

"The symbolism is all Coptic, Ma." Saren traced the outline of the stamped symbol of the book within the collection. "This is the red seal of his adorable one, the seal of Mary of Magdalene."

Jumping to her feet, Ma hurried around the table. "Yes, Pa would know who could read this; he has many friends from foreign lands."

"My Nan would have read these. And I don't know if she still lives." Tears fell quietly to Saren's lap.

"Then that is what we are to do, Saren. We must go to Pa. Go to Oxford and help him get out of prison." Ma clapped her hands in glee.

Saren relaxed and reached for her cup of broth.

Laying her hand upon Saren's, "We can learn the meaning there. I know of a Coptic book of Pa's. Come." The women hurried to fetch the ancient text, their urgency escalating.

"A trip must be necessary to retrieve Pa from prison, Saren. And to learn the meaning of these books." Ma rushed to Saren. "We shall take a trip to Oxford. There, we may find counsel and help from William." With nothing for Ma to occupy her hands, she took to folding and refolding her apron. I struggle with going on the road to Oxford," Ma confessed. "Would you be willing to travel alone while I remain here?"

"Of course, I've made it this far. I do fear leaving you, however." The women exchanged smiles of understanding. For, leaving Ma behind was their only financial possibility, though Saren would have loved to have her company had she her choice.

Knowing that Sir Henry Percy had taken her translated copies of the Bibles from their hiding place on the rocky shore of the River Thames, Saren now felt his eyes upon her every moment and imagined him one pace behind her every step.

Though once charming, Sir Percy's sullen manner now felt like the evil that it indeed was. Wicked.

Saren ducked among the oncoming pedestrians, trying feverishly to shake his presence, to no avail. Without delivering her latest parcel, she ventured home. Stepping beyond the cover of solid crates smelling of stale linen. Saren removed her unforgotten ebony blade from her boot.

The ever-warm stone rested heavy in her hand as she returned to her pilgrimage to the Wynch house. "Give me courage, if nothing more," she whispered to herself as she left the safety of the crowded street.

Falling into a deliberate rhythmic stride, Saren began to walk cautiously, and her pride returned. Not one moment too soon, the hedge beyond her back cloaked her ambush.

Saren heard the rushing of steps and crunching of grass seconds before seeing the large-cloaked figure heading toward her. Sir Percy locked eyes with her as he said, "You will give me your father's secrets, now!"

Saren's instinct was savage. Not fleeing nor screaming, but with her sharp blade cloaked behind her shawl, she charged at her pursuer in like speed as he. The duo collided and fell to the ground, Saren lying beneath her attacker. His eyes were wild beyond fear; he fought.

Saren averted her gaze and held fast to his frame and her stone blade that would remain forever lodged in his heart. His fighting ceased. She left him upon the earth as the red pool grew beneath him. His eyes grew cold.

Rounding the hedge, she kneeled to steady her trembling. With her eyes now closed, she remained in prayer, "My Father who art in heaven, please forgive me for the taking of this man's life. I am sorry. And now, I am safe," she sobbed uncontrollably, leaped to her feet, and ran for the home that she now knew.

◈　　◈　　◈

Using all the family's savings, Ma and Saren found her fare to Oxford. She would travel three days and two nights to aid in the release of William's father.

They had discovered the untruth that had passed down over the generations—lies that had stolen hopes, smashed dreams, and broken hearts. The truth that must be shouted from the mountaintops, that friends and holy men had died trying to tell. The truth that encompassed the wisdom of God being far greater than the sacrament of his body, his death, and his resurrection.

Before departing London—where there has been too much pain and suffering, too much death—Saren smiled her best smile for Ma. "If we save other innocents from dying without hearing the Lord's truth, if we die for speaking the truth, then we have succeeded."

Ma held her close in her warm embrace. "We have much work ahead, Saren. I hope you are well." Ma pulled her away to see her face. "You can find what we need. You were sent to me for this purpose, don't you know? Please help find Pa's release before he, too, is murdered."

"This is my intention." Saren squeezed Ma's shoulders, refusing to say goodbye. Instead, she said, "We will be together again."

CHAPTER SIXTEEN

Guidance from Purgatory

He played for the departed, the hungry, and the falsely accused. No longer was Charles playing for peace but for mercy. There would be no death, nor dying, here this day as he followed Ma Wynch and his daughter through the rain as they departed from one another.

The downpour ricocheted from the puddles, serenading from below as it fell from above. Charles cast his glance ahead for refuge for his daughter.

He strolled, watching as she huddled into a dry pub, the perfect place to play a lively tune of refuge on his pipes.

❖   ❖   ❖

The night approached, Saren could find no lodging; her only option for shelter was the pub on the outskirts of the city, where she had found shelter from the rain while waiting for the next cart to Oxford.

The tavern was crammed from wall to wall with patrons—some regulars, some thirsty, some in need of a roof to cover them, and most desperate for human interaction and a happy heart.

The rain brought not only water but also a downpour of sorrow and gloom. For many days, the sun had not shone or shared its warmth through the haze.

Nevertheless, here at Marion's Pub, there was cheer and hope, as if a beam of sun shone directly through the clouds over the pub's thatched roof. Voices sang and cheered and laughed. Sweet smoke escaped above into the rafters, and the floor shook with rowdy stomps.

The aroma of roasted duck touched Saren's nose. She smiled because the shelter served her well. Saren crouched at the corner table, her head draped with Ma's worn coat. She clutched her bag of books and belongings close to her chest.

A woman brought a bowl of soup and bread to the table and eyed her flirtatiously, assuming she was a lad due to her short hair and trousers. She ate silently, for voices would not have been heard over the roar of the pub to allow her to reveal her true gender. The warmth and commotion of the place brought her cheer despite being so far from her new home.

Saren ate her soup and sipped her ale. The warmth of the room intensified, soon, Saren was longing for a place to rest her weary head.

She struggled not to close her eyes, for the possibility of being robbed was real; however, she dozed across the bench as the rain continued its incessant fury beyond the doors.

Morning light would not loom soon enough. Saren had never consumed such quantities of ale. Her hand was held fast across her head, and the crease between her brows told of her misery.

She walked from Marion's Pub. Only puddles remained of the rain upon the saturated earth. No wrath fell from the clouds that lingered heavy as she felt her way through the streets toward the cart.

Mud clung to Saren's shoes, which grew heavier with every step.

The coach to take her into Oxford was loaded and waiting as she neared. The last leg of her destination was over in no time. Saren slept while the cart rocked and bumped her as she dreamed.

Father sat, stone-like, upon the shore. He watched out to sea for something or perhaps someone. Calling to him, Saren ran toward him, though he never heard her. His mouth moved, but she could not hear what he was saying. He spoke with a woman there upon the beach.

She wore a white cape over her head as if attempting to conceal her pale skin and ashen hair. She looked to Saren, smiling. Saren did not recognize her face.

Upon arriving at Oxford, Saren found clear blue skies and warmer air.

The people of the inn opened their doors with a welcome cheer. The city bustled with loud conversation and the traffic of prosperity. To the alien newcomer, the hospitality was more welcoming than London's bustle. As different and suspicious as it was, one could not help but succumb to the festivity.

Her funds, however, rapidly dwindling. Saren's thoughts migrated to the concern of her inevitable journey home and her longing for Ma's company. The homeward trek became her obsession. With an unsettled task to summon help to secure Pa Wynch's release, Saren's priority was to find William. And, perhaps, with William's presence here, his pa's release would be timely.

Saren shared no real conversation with the keepers of the inn that first afternoon. She rummaged through the Coptic translations she had carried from home, recognizing her need for more resources. Finally deciding to act, she attempted to visit Wycliffe's home, which he kept in Oxford. Sighing an exaggerated breath, she remarked inwardly that *there stood no reason why anyone would be granted entrance to the Wycliffe house. The mere mention of it means heresy.*

She could not have been more right. The keeper of the first home that had been the reverend's refused her in every regard. The mention of the name at once caused mounting suspicions. At last, Saren attempted entrance to the college campus, where a great library was housed.

Saren slept her first nights at Oxford in style, treated with the respect and friendliness of nobility. Breakfast was exquisite. Such flattery, Saren had never been privileged to. The lifestyle, charming as it was, was far too restraining and muffling for the young lady's free spirit. And it was just as well.

Upon returning from her first day's attempt to locate information about Pa Wynch's release, she found that her belongings were heaped in the inn's front lobby.

She had been expelled from her suite.

In the firmest, nastiest tone, as Saren tried to question why her belongings were cast out, the innkeeper declared, "You are to leave at once. We have no rooms available for Lollards."

"Aye, I can't afford your fees another night, anyway," Saren rebuked.

Saren grabbed her belongings and stood facing the busy streets as if looking for directions.

What more can I do but return home? But I mustn't—I have only begun. Saren shut her eyes to the noon sun and searched for lodging options.

She maneuvered among the streets near the river Cherwell; though it was pretty, the smell of waste and garbage rose from the stagnant waters. She was quickly encouraged back to the streets and located a small, welcoming pub. Seated indoors, she found the smell of rising bread, ale, and burning wood.

There, Saren was waited on by an aged man with a slumped spine. He shuffled about the small parlor, delivering plates and cups to the patrons. He offered a cheery smile despite missing most of his gnarled teeth.

A pair of younger men sat down at a table near her. They carried satchels of books, wore simple clothes, and carried a grace about them that only the clean-shaven, manicured man can.

"Good day, Lad." The tallest of the men gave Saren a polite tip of his brushed leather cap.

The old, bent waiter returned to her table with a tray of bread and warm mead. He shuffled about them, fixing and fidgeting, and displayed his hideous teeth with a hearty smile. As the old waiter bumbled around, Saren kept her thoughts to herself.

All the while, the two men relaxed at the neighboring table, carrying on a conversation audible to all who cared to listen.

"The monies owed to the lender ought not be subject to the Crown's tax, save the interest earned by it," the slenderer man said.

The conversation of political problems meant little to Saren, yet she sat, absently listening. The gentlemen's conversation changed course when the plump man shared the strife he had encountered en route to Berkley. His eyes grew large as he told his friend, "We were traveling in broad daylight." He set his cup of mead on the table and went on. "There were perhaps ten men. Boys, really. They rode up alongside us, keeping us in a small formation. Many of them had bows and several knives."

He dabbed his hatless head with his kerchief. "The bandits chanted, 'Give up your purses, or we take your life.'

Again and again, they would shout this." Wiping his mouth with his kerchief, he concluded, "One dares not travel without an armed escort or being fully armed and ready to fight for one's life."

After a deep sip from his goblet, he said, "They stopped us below a knoll, made us take off our shoes, and give all of our coins to them." He scanned the room to see if everyone was listening and concluded, "They took us for everything, left us with nothing. I say, Lad." The stout man's eyes looked to Saren. "Be warned if you travel the country. I shan't think of what might become of a lass at nightfall in the woods." He looked to Saren as he spoke.

Saren turned her gaze away from his as the heat flushed her face.

"Aye, sir. I keep with good company," she retorted in her most resounding voice to the young man's heavy stare, then went back to tasting her tepid drink.

The chatty men finally departed, leaving Saren to contemplate her overwhelming task of fetching William and freeing Pa Wynch from his Oxford prison. First, though, the contents of her father's sacred books must be revealed to her. This once-forbidden message was now her destined treasure, and she was to stop at nothing until the truth was protected.

The afternoon was nearly over, and lodging became the first item on her agenda. As she prepared to leave, she paid the old man for his fine hospitality and asked, "Do you know of any room for rent nearby?"

Without a word, the bent and crippled man waved across the way, his smile never betraying him.

Saren went in the direction he had pointed and inquired about a room.

At twilight, she took up lodging in a room above a dingy pub. The space was small, but the price was reasonable, so she took it gladly. Here, she could afford to stay for as long as needed.

The small bed of straw was heavily blanketed and well made, aside from gaping holes protruding and mouse droppings littering the blankets.

She had unpacked her belongings and was settling in when it started. The brawls began like friendly scuffles at first. Then, the scuffling grew abusive as the night fell around. The crashing of barrels and shouting was ceaseless in the tavern below. She would find no sleep at this new lodging.

Saren rose and dressed long before dawn. Taking out her sacred book, she voiced to herself, *Come. What am I waiting for? There is no time to lose. I have a plan.* She hurried out, leaving the noise of the riots and the mice for later.

◈   ◈   ◈

The wind ceased sometime in the night. Having only slept the short morning hours, Nan rose to earn their keep above Marion's Pub.

She was close to finding Saren. Saren had been here and slept on the benches. Like Nan and John Aston, Saren found shelter from the rains here.

The cleaning was taxing on Nan's weary bones, but the food was good and the shelter sublime. Nan quickly befriended the one young barmaid and learned that Saren had stopped here, dressed as a boy and frightened, to wait for passage to Oxford not long ago. Relieved at knowing Saren's destination, Nan and Mr. Aston were bound for Oxford.

Nan kept her blade near and studied the faces of every cloaked man. As relieved as she was to have gained knowledge of Saren's whereabouts, she suspected Lord Percy would have the same knowledge.

◆   ◆   ◆

CHAPTER SEVENTEEN

A Companion

The quiet of the empty streets was welcoming the moments before dawn when only morning stars remained. Saren walked on toward the Oxford library.

She held tightly to the candle she had taken from the dingy room. Neither guards nor sentries stood anticipating this early hour's library patronage. While in the shadows of the towering building, Saren walked about, navigating her surroundings. I shan't stay more than an hour, she coaxed herself forward in search of an entrance to the building.

All doors were fastened, deadbolted from within. There was one door below ground Saren had not tried. Beyond a narrow rock wall, a steep hallway dropped to the iron-fired door.

Saren made peace with the iron gaud, saw herself beyond its grip, and wiggled in.

Before stepping through the darkened room, Saren surveyed the nearby candelabra and lit the wick of her candle.

Once in the building, she left the door ajar, promising herself to return to this spot in a moment, maybe two, after looking around for clues to obtain a Coptic resource. At most, she yearned to discover where she could deliver her family's sacred collection of books for safekeeping. She hurried through the cold, dank darkness before she could hesitate.

The floors creaked and popped beneath Saren's dainty stride as she hurried away from the building's abyss. Books lined every space above ground.

The light from Saren's candle shone enough to create her shadow, magnifying her silhouette upon the white walls. Tables stood around the great room, and chairs she knocked into time after time. Having a feel for the room in the light of day would have helped her in the unfamiliar surroundings, though what she desperately sought remained elusive.

She worked her way around the floor once, touching the countless books delicately. She had no time now; Saren longed to pick up each book and read from its fine pages. She spotted several thick, heavy books splayed open across the main counter of the building. Saren trailed her candle's light near them and memorized the lay of the room. She hurried back to check that her door remained ajar.

"I may have found something of use. At least a Latin dictionary that may be useful," Saren told herself. I may need to borrow a few things to read in the light of day. She began to enjoy her own company.

She walked silently through the shadows, then returned to the display case to read on.

She had found several Latin Bibles and two mysterious scrolls. She hesitated before sitting to read, but the quiet candlelit room was a welcome place to begin. She selected one scroll and one book, then returned the others to their rightful places among the exquisite collection for another night's research. Saren read what she could, making notes on her own tablet of her discoveries, and hastened to aid in Pa Wynch's release.

The candle burned up quickly, leaving but a puddle of light for her to contend with.

Saren returned the books, pushed her chair back, and left the building as she'd found it.

Having found ancient Coptic symbols, like those upon her gift from Joseph upon the Al-Aoura, Saren knew she must come again to compare them to Joseph's book. Saren stopped, resting her satchel upon the earth, she turned scooting the heavy door across the dirt. Finding success; she smiled a sleepy smile and maneuvered it closed.

She returned to a much quieter pub than she had left. Climbing the steps to her mouse-infested room, she had no energy for thinking. Sleep found her quickly, and the scurrying of tiny feet about the room did not disturb.

❖　　❖　　❖

The bustle and voices of the street woke Saren late in the morning. She was eager to read the work she had scribbled by candlelight before dawn. Saren smiled at finding Coptic symbols on her family's secret book when roused by a coughing fit.

"Oh, dear me," exclaimed Saren. "Whatever will I do if I come down with the flux?"

Saren focused on her mission to release Pa and find Will. She was Pa's only hope now.

The wind grew restless outside in harmony with the late afternoon crowd in the pub below. Saren went down to inquire about directions from the patrons. Numerous gents were willing to show her where she could locate Oxford's seminary and William's lodging. Though a sharply dressed lad slurred, "Ye ain't getten pass em doors. At's empossible."

The seminary at Oxford rose grotesquely among the buildings. Saren attempted the best impersonation of a boy that she could muster, for she knew beyond a doubt that she would be forcefully removed if her identity was revealed.

Speaking, therefore, was not an option. Saren returned to her room above the tavern and drafted another letter for William. Assuming that others would read it before he received it, she wrote so that only Will would comprehend. She wrote:

Dear William,

I am certain that your work and study are as lengthy as mine. Be it known Ma Wynch is now residing at home alone, for my work has brought me away and closer to the source.

I am looking to find the timely release of one very dear. And I work nightly nearby, surrounded by glorious books.

Yours truly, S.

Dressed in her borrowed boyish attire and wearing a new cap, she delivered her message to William at Oxford Seminary and returned to the pub.

Life in the pub erupted as she studied.

Saren began her trek to the library hours earlier than the previous morning's adventure, escaping the loud havoc of the pub.

She knew where she was going, and Saren knew what she was looking for this night—a schedule of lynchings, something, or someone to help Pa Wynch, and perhaps a Coptic-English dictionary. . .

Sitting at the grand table beneath the candle's flicker, Saren read silently from the pale pages, a full moon rose over the building, casting unfamiliar shadows upon the floor.

The library's quiet, resting heavy upon her like fog, cracked as Saren abruptly moved her chair across the polished floor.

Before having a moment to ponder the words she read, there came a scuffling of feet upon the floor sending Saren into panic.

Saren stuffed the news bulletin among her belongings and left the ornate Coptic Bible open on the table. She sheltered her flame and fled to find a hiding place, leaving the chairs askew. Locating a hiding place before reaching the bottom stairwell, she hid.

She could hear quickly approaching footsteps and remained hidden. The nearing bustle went from low and mournful growls to sudden alarming yowls and yelps.

A bristly, homely, and hungry stray mutt had discovered the door left ajar.

With a sigh and a smile Saren said, "I shall call you Charles after Father. Charlie, for short." Then, she went back to her studies.

Saren traced the Coptic symbols with her finger from page to page. The thin ink left perfect, clean, and crisp as though no one before her had read the pages of the treasured Bible. Just as her father's Bibles had inspired her to write, to study, to translate, to share the words, she wrote in the candle's light. Her father's work had not been in vain. His lessons—far more numerous than all her endeavors—had all been successful. Here alone, with her mangy Charlie asleep at her feet, she matched her English Bible verses to the Coptic symbols that remained open on the table.

There will be continued strife to spread these English Bibles. *The struggle will be justified with the revelation of The Book of Sophia of Jesus Christ,* Saren decided. Yawning, she returned all the books she had removed from the shelves. She was nearly about to pinch her candle's flame when Charlie rose and stretched, his haunches sticking up behind him. A slight wag of his tail gave Saren reason to smile.

"Come now, we must find a meal before we both faint. Oh," Saren stammered. "I failed to return the news bulletin tucked among my own." She clutched her hand across her mouth.

She sighed. "It shan't be missed for one day. We will return it tomorrow." She shrugged and walked out beyond the great door. There, she knelt, talking to the shaggy mongrel.

Saren read on through the hours until dawn, though she hated to break her momentum, "I feel as if I am under a spell, little Charles." She broke her concentration to rustle his mangy head. "I can't seem to want to come up for breath. There is so much knowledge to be had. I shan't dare begin to explain what I have discovered until I am certain of what I read," she told her new friend before hurrying off again to her work.

The title of the third of her father's sacred books, "The Apocryphon of John," took Saren hours to translate using Pa Wynch's ancient Coptic writing. She first had to understand the meaning of the symbols. The project was a daunting task. The title, translated and transcribed by her hand, inspired her to work into the morning.

Each hour that passed, each word written, showed Saren more clearly the need to protect the words she revealed.

"And his thought performed a deed, and she came forth, namely she who had appeared before him in the shine of his light, she transcribed. *"This is the first power which was before all of them which came forth from his mind, she is the forethought of the All - her light shines like his light - the perfect power which is the image of the invisible, virginal Spirit who is perfect. She became the womb of everything, for it is she who is prior to them all, the Mother-Father, the first man, the holy Spirit, the thrice-male, the thrice-powerful, the thrice-named androgynous one."* [4] Saren wrote. And wrote.

When the kitchen noises below reminded her tummy that it was empty, Saren looked up from her work, fearing eyes upon her or perhaps the presence of the late author Reverend Wycliffe himself visiting her from his wet grave of the river Swift, where the Church had thrown his ashes in protest of his heresies, to share with her this transcription. Her heart's patter turned to pounding.

Saren reached for her canine companion, thumping his tail on the dingy floor. She could not help but smile as her uneasiness at being alone ceased with having her newfound companion.

CHAPTER EIGHTEEN

Choices

William carried his cumbersome stack of books and manuscripts across the soggy grass of the seminary courtyard as the cloaked summer sun fell from the sky.

The tedious work was not difficult nor tasking, he thought to himself. Why, then, can I not keep my focus on my studies?

William approached the dormitory as a pod of older students marched, chatting. One student, smiling and shy, held the door for William as he maneuvered his books past. Never making eye contact with William, the shy lad raced after his friends without a "Hello."

William reached his room and was grateful to find it vacant of his roommate. He longed to catch up on his studies, which he seemed to sit and stare at for hours to find no joy in his tasks.

He sat alone, with one leather-bound book open before him, his mind clouded with thoughts and refusing to relinquish any space for new knowledge.

"What is the matter with me?" William breathed a heavy moan. "I must feel as those older boys look?" he thought aloud. "Not happy." William stood and began pacing. "Well, the one boy was not happy. The others, perhaps." He grabbed his jacket and hurried beyond his dormitory to locate James, a fellow student.

The sun had set and started trying to penetrate the growing clouds when William located the older student sitting quietly among his peers in the parish hall.

"James, you are James, correct?" William asked with a shy smile to match the other students.

"Yes, William," the classmate answered. His eyes filled with questions.

"Good evening to you, friend. I wanted to thank you properly for holding the dormitory door earlier." William shifted his feet upon the smooth floor of the foyer. "James, I'm struggling with my studies, and I hope that you can help me." William looked around at the other faces talking. And to James's panicked expression.

"Why do you imagine that I might help ye, William? Don't you see the struggles that I manage each day?" James stammered with a gulp.

"No, I can't see that at all, James. I know nothing of you second- and third-year students." William gnawed his lower lip, trying to resist his nervous pacing. "I simply recognize myself in you and thought, perhaps, that between us, we could figure out our troubles."

With a gentle sigh, James asked, "Shall we go for a stroll?" He dropped his clasped hands and led the way across the great hall.

They had walked in silence for long, deliberate moments, each young lad lost in his own thought, when William and James both began speaking at the same time.

"It does not matter...," said William.

"I cannot keep...," said James, then continued. "I am a fair student. I try every day to do my very best." He averted his eyes to concentrate on his steps but stopped. "What we speak here must never be shared with another. Do you understand?" he asked William.

"Yes, of course, James. I promise. I need your help." "Are you easily distracted? Having trouble sleeping?

Barely making passing marks?" James questioned.

"Well, yes. My marks are well enough, but I can't get any of my studies done properly. I am here in body, but my head is anywhere and everywhere else."

"Yes, we have the same conditions. And I know what it is, William." James began walking again, mostly to give his eyes something new to focus upon. "There is nothing either of us can do to remedy our despair."

"What despair, James? I'm not troubled or hurt. I just cannot focus my attentions on my studies."

"Precisely!" James burst out, grabbing William by the shoulders, and spinning him to face him. "Can you not see where your heart is? It is no more here than mine, friend."

"What are you saying?"

"You came to me for help. Now that's what I'm giving, William." James dropped his grip from William's shoulders and smiled a broken smile. "My heart, it belongs in Coventry, to Mary. Not here."

William stepped back and away from James's grasp upon his shoulders, and his eyes widened. "Oh," he breathed at last. *"My heart and my mind are Saren's."*

James heard William's words, "And here we are, brother, confined to these, the Lord's walls." He motioned to the high stone fences surrounding the seminary.

"Yes, we are confined. But by only a stone wall. Nothing more, James. Why have I not seen this before? You are right. My heart does not belong here." William remained bewildered in his thoughts and began again to pace as he spoke. "The walls are only a physical barricade. Our hearts are free—this I know." Looking to James, he added, "Are not we given free choice to choose, our free will, given by God? Is not that true? Though some would not want us knowing such truths."

James stepped up beside William, and they walked side by side as he spoke. "Yes, William. God wants us here, and only by our own free will."

"Yes."

"Then I shall return to my Mary at once."

"And I to my Saren."

CHAPTER NINETEEN

Reunion

The dingy tavern below was not as booming with venom as it had been during the previous night's brawl. They sat among the broken chairs and tables, feasting on pottage and thick, warm ale. The people who worked here at the pub were no better kept than the building. One young lad appeared to have been involved in the most recent night's ruckus. Saren could not help but smile at the young man's maimed and broken nose, for his cracked and swollen knuckles ensured that someone else in town had a face looking much the same.

Eating a meal, Saren shared with her new shaggy friend, who refused to disappear. He lay at her feet, thumping his tail against her leg. No one refused him as he slunk in behind her, so there the mutt remained.

Saren took out her last remaining English Bible, unintentionally reading in a soft voice.

The room grew quiet around her. Saren read on, ignorant of the attention she had found from the introduction to Wycliffe's New Testament.

All eyes in the tavern lay on Saren. She closed the book on the table as if to take back what she had just read aloud and keep herself from reading.

The broken-nosed barman requested with no more than a whisper, "Please, read on, Lad. You be in fine company with us." There were cheers all around in agreement.

A fellow gent, who sat leaning on the bar, removed his cap and came nearer Saren's table. He sauntered over, holding his cap loosely between his fingers. He asked briskly, "May I sit with you, Lass?"

"Um, yes." Saren became cognizant of the savage scar upon his cheek. She hesitated.

The shaggy mongrel hurried over to the stranger for a pat.

The peculiar man stooped to pet the dog before locating a chair. Once he pulled a chair near, he offered his hand to Saren. "Good day. My name's John Aston of Braxton. Where do you bring that book from? If you do not mind my asking? Why, they're all but destroyed here at Oxford."

"Why, yes," she hesitated. "It is not mine, but one that once belonged to an old friend," Saren whispered. He reached across the table to fondle the book, but Saren pulled it close, catching his eyes from across the table.

His eyes were charcoal gray, like soot from the morning fire. The thick, smooth scar graced his left cheekbone, running outward toward his scalp.

Saren removed the book and looked around for reassurance.

"You have no reason to fear, Saren Eadwine of Northumberland, My Lady." The mysterious man attempted a smile. "I would like to offer you my help, if I may," he said as he reached down to pat the dog again.

"I could use some help," she responded as she stood, trying to repress her wavering voice from alarm at him knowing her name.

He stood from the table. Saren remained with her meal and ale.

"It belonged to our late friend Sir Oldcastle of London," she spoke the truth. "We have come to clear my friend's pa," she stammered. "Mr. James Wynch. He was only the messenger." Saren swallowed hard and regained her seat.

"Won't you please join me?" he asked. "Your Nan has been looking for you. I may know where you may find Mr. Wynch, though we must hurry."

Mr. Aston stood. stood. Saren took a few sips from her mug, set it on the table, and, leaving her uneaten meal, she followed him.

The wind had ceased for the first moments in days. Debris and rubbish filled the streets. Saren hurried her steps into a gentle trot to keep close to Mr. Aston. Charlie, though, trotted ahead as though he knew their destination well.

People busied past as Saren studied her surroundings, hoping to remember her steps back to her lodging.

Just as she located one recognizable landmark, Mr. Aston ducked behind a heavy planked door. He held it open just enough for Saren to follow.

She hesitated a moment longer before asking, "Where did you meet my Nan? And how will I find Mr. Wynch?"

"I'm getting to that, My Lady." Mr. Aston scanned the room filled with his loyal followers. "We are all the Lollard Society, Wycliffe's followers or 'poor priests.' The others have all recanted and been forgiven of their crimes to save their own necks."

The great room beyond the door smelled of stale air. Mr. Aston located two candles on a vacant hearth, lit them, and placed them in stone candelabras inscribed with Hebrew tablature.

Mr. Aston opened a worn Bible. "The trumpet thus becomes associated with the advent of the moment of chastisement. Apocalyptic in its severity, known as the Day of the Lord," he read.

Saren listened on as the priest of the Lollard Church gave his sermon taken from further passages of Jeremiah: "' And the blowing of the trumpets whose sound disclosed God's presence, Strophar like a horn.'"

Father Aston gave his sermon, though brief, to Saren and the few men who had followed from the bar and now stood among them at the small tranquil church, where no light dared penetrate the windows, no Latin dared be uttered, no gold would be collected from its patrons, Saren could feel God's presence flood the room.

"The translations of Wycliffe's New Testament, both the first and the second editions, mind you, include the Epistle to the Laodiceans." John watched Saren for her recognition of this. When no one spoke up, he went on. "Rejected by the Biblical canon, perhaps, at the close of the third century. Some read the Epistle to the Laodiceans, but it is rejected by everyone, De viris ill." Mr. Aston left the room a moment and returned with a book in his hands. John inhaled deeply. "Saren, the crown, and the church don't want the people to know they don't have to pay for the Lord's forgiveness." Looking into her eyes, he added, "The grace of God is free for us all." He closed the book and laid it upon the makeshift altar.

"The Epistle to the Laodiceans is the fifteenth Epistle of Paul written to the church of the Laodiceans, and thus rejected by the church and deemed radical." John dropped his hands and sighed before continuing. "The letters were destroyed; the masses will never know their meaning. The books we carry are deemed heresy because they invoke the wisdom of God. His message. Not so much the messenger. If the church accepts the rest as scripture, they must also accept the books of Sophia. Yes, wisdom as much as Jesus." Mr. Aston nodded. "God is all. Father, Son, and Mother. The church has control and will stop at nothing to protect their patriarch."

The books that she had in her possession, the church sought to destroy before the people could gain knowledge given by Jesus himself.

Saren nodded in agreement with Mr. Aston's words, reminding herself, "He knows nothing of the sacred treasures that I possess." The crushing of brittle pages with the closing of Mr. Aston's book had stolen Saren's attention, and she looked to the familiar yet haunting book. What she recognized there upon the table took her breath away.

Before John could offer words, she removed the book from the table. Opening its cover, she confirmed what she already knew. "This is one of my father's Bibles. His hand's script," she cried.

The door of the chapel hurled open as Nan could no longer be restrained from taking her wee granddaughter tight into her arms. Word had reached her that Saren had been found and was safe back at the makeshift chapel with Mr. Aston.

"My prayers have been answered at last—my Saren girl is here." Nan rushed to Saren. Both women, sobbing, wrapped their arms tight in an embrace.

"I'm so sorry for leaving you, Nan," Saren cried.

"There, there, child. I expected nothing less. I have only come to warn you of the pursuers that are seeking your family's secret. Lord Percy and his son, Henry." Nan held Saren an arm's length away to see into her eyes.

"I know. Not to worry about Sir Henry Percy. He is no longer a concern." Saren shut her eyes. "Lord Percy has crossed my path once before…" her eyes widened.

"Yes, and we are here now together to help protect the secret books from falling into his evil hands," Saren added. "Now, we must secure these secrets away until our world is ready to know the Lord's truth. I fear many more lives shall be lost in any attempt to share such truths today."

CHAPTER TWENTY

A Lynching

Morning slowly turned into day. The sky began to weep as Saren, Nan, and Mr. Aston made their way across busy streets and between rickety old buildings. Mr. Aston's feet kept moving effortlessly, though Saren's had to move twice as fast to keep up.

She had to grab Mr. Aston's shirt sleeve and say, "Please, can we slow our pace?"

"The lynching happens at precisely noon, as is always the case. Make haste, lass. Nan, meet us at the city center."

Saren clung to her father's pages like his life ebbed through the lines. The cough she had acquired sitting in the cold library was wreaking havoc upon her now as she hacked between breaths. Saren's feet grew heavy with the burden of interfering in a lynching, though her heart was made much lighter in knowing that her Nan had sought her all this time.

Mr. Aston slowed his brisk pace but never stopped to wait for her or for Nan.

Saren hurried to catch up to the long-legged Mr. Aston and followed behind more than ten paces, never catching up with him entirely.

The late July sun in Oxford is often disguised or cloaked by heavy strata. This summer morning was no different from the rainy days that came before. They led James Wynch, William's father, from the courtrooms, his hands bound behind his back, his hair slicked back into a tight knot. Yet he smiled a smile of autonomy, of a man who knows his innocence and his duty. His cheer was catching and could have been contagious, had not the outcome of the event been preordained.

Mr. Aston led them behind a row of businesses past a worn and rundown chapel. The shutters had been ripped from their hinges, and the mortar between the walls' stones crumbled in patches.

The sky misted upon them like dust now. Puddles lingered on the ground, rippled by the gentle breeze. They made their way toward an ancient door, too old to repair but in dire need of attention.

William placed his few important belongings upon his bedroll. He'd never been without a destination in mind before. Deep in his soul, he knew he had been wrong to accept this role at the seminary.

There were no words that could express his gratitude for the opportunity given by Sir Oldcastle. He had learned of Sir Oldcastle's demise only days previous.

William feared for his father, for Saren, and for his ma's fate. Sitting and studying here behind this stone wall was no longer a place for him. William found James, and together, they went to the cathedral to speak with the bishop and pray if necessary. William stopped at the priory to see if he had received any letters.

The collection from Saren was alarming, and William immediately opened the most recent. He learned she was here in Oxford, working nights at the library just down the street from his dormitory. He read about his father's hearing and sentencing, to be fulfilled at any one of the lynchings this month.

The noon sun climbed higher, penetrating the mist. William found his way to the city center with his possessions rolled in his blanket and tied upon his back. The unread letters from his beloved tucked beneath his rope belt. A loose crowd trickled into the center.

Pa Wynch shook his head. Laughing, he whispered, "I am not guilty of crimes of heresy toward God. Only your church's laws will see me hang." He spoke again, weak as his body had become. "I will not tell of any other men who speak against this evil. Have me executed, and the names of those fellow knights who fight for righteousness' sake will be safely taken to my grave." He had witnessed godly men, spanning the years across King Henry's kingdom, accused of heresy, all unjustly accused by the church's laws, not the laws of scripture. To him, the crime was in recanting and abiding by the church's unholy laws. His trial had been set during the same week as King Henry Bolingbroke's coronation, though no trial had come. Alone, he had prayed, confined in the tower at Oxford's prison through the summer months.

The guards had removed the shackles from his feet the night prior to his execution, perhaps as a gesture of kindness. Now, they escorted him to the city center.

The city's center filled with people for this execution, the social event, the entertainment provided by the church—which all were required to attend. The clear sky now filled with heavy, dark rain clouds rolling and bumping, pushing each other together as if fighting for a place to witness this wrath of man. An older guard stood near Pa Wynch, and they placed him at the pole and fastened him. His fellow guardsmen were whispering and chatting among themselves. Turning, he asked the crowd gathered, "Does anyone have last words to be voiced on Mr. James Wynch's behalf?"

The silence among the people was one that Saren knew well. She had not expected less.

The wind, knocking the clouds about overhead, subtly descended upon the scene. Gently, they appeared to stir the air, and the occasional blow of debris from the earth sent the air spiraling. The breeze gained momentum, like a crescendo, and the wind hurled itself upon the crowd, keeping the flames from being lit.

A gust rattled the window's shutters, and people rushed about the streets, grabbing belongings to keep them from blowing away.

The wind-arsenal brought with it a wet blitz that caused Saren to pull her shawl up around her shoulders. She shivered. Her chill would have been just as strong without the storm; she noticed Lord Percy in the crowd looking for his treasure, which was now coupled with the vendetta to pay for the taking of his son's life.

Mr. Aston, taking notice of this man's presence, stepped obtrusively between Lord Percy and Saren, obscuring his line of vision.

For the first time in many cycles of the moon, Charles had lost his temper and lashed out in anger at this malice of man. The angrier he became, the more hatred he hurled in the direction of the executioners, the louder his music grew, and the stronger the winds became.

He looked about and saw what was about to unfold before him. Charles knew that he was not as powerful as all their evil, but he was much wiser. Recognizing this, he used his most powerful weapon. Charles played his gift. Charles gathered his pipes about him, took one more look at the man bound to the stake, and then located his daughter clutching her shawl about her. Squeezing his bellows, he played.

The bellows' squall fanned the wind just as it had begun, and the elder guard left his perch upon the mount. When Charles's piping started, people clambered about gathering their possessions, coats, and children. All eyes looked toward its source, but there was no musician to be found, only the serenade of a storm. The music came rich to their ears as if direct from heaven. There was no explanation for the music's source nor certainty of any music bounding across the winds. The raging winds only encouraged the crowd to take cover.

Saren stepped forward, her hair swimming about her head. She walked to Pa Wynch, their eyes never parting.

"Yes, I am compelled to speak this day on Pa Wynch's behalf." She cast her gaze across the countless Christian faces, hurrying away to find cover from the storm. "Let it be known that God is watching this day as you attempt to murder this man. James Wynch has shared the word of God for years. He fought to tell the truth of God's own lips. Not the church's, nor man's." She recognized familiar books of her own hand among those piled beneath Pa Wynch. Nothing remained for her to transcribe; no words were left to glean insight from, for now, her voice would serve her.

The first books were set ablaze just as the winds caught the flames, fanning the smoke into another tyrant storm.

There were no longer books to share, no babe to console. Saren's spirit was breaking. *If her father had known what he had entrusted her with, would he have given her an alternate destination?* His sacred book brushing her flesh, she pondered.

The flames struggled; no life would be taken. Only the display of one man, though not innocent, accused of unjust crimes.

The storm intensified, and spectators fled. The guards that remained stood with their backs to the torrential rains, faces covered. Mr. Aston clutched Saren's shoulder as she pulled him toward Pa Wynch, saying, "Quickly. We must move fast."

His arms first were freed and pressed upon Saren's back as Mr. Aston bent to unbind his ankles.

William, having faced the storm and witnessed the opportunity, stood poised. When he recognized Saren's voice, he was there to unfasten his pa's wrists.

Not a soul remained among the witnesses to protest their rescue. As Saren held the bound man from falling, the flames from the hand-copied Bibles below licked her skin, and smoke filled their lungs. They did not linger. The wind roared down upon the scattering crowd, and music intensified from the heavens. The lingering crowd dispersed, and Saren steadied the weak man. Without a moment to spare, Saren beat at her smoldering skirt to swat out the flames. The guards looked on briefly, but soon they, too, departed from the storm, contrary to the one protest from Lord Percy. Saren aided Pa Wynch to shelter from the storm. Few words were spoken between them, though the poor man knew nothing of Saren's identity. Only occasional warm smiles were exchanged between him and his son.

With the gnashing of the storm, they departed silently into the rain and found their way to the edge of town, the mangy mongrel following obediently.

The winds raged into the twilight hour, lifting sand loose from the ground and hurling it against their flesh. Saren held fast to Pa Wynch's hand as they made their way through the streets full of commotion and panic. Babies cried, and mamas hurried. Through all the chaos, Saren denied the urgency as she steadily marched this unknown yet familiar man to safety.

Taking refuge among the carthorses' house, built of an ageless corral, the newly acquainted party consoled each other, William holding tight to Saren's hand.

"Pa, my name is Saren Eadwine, daughter of Sir Charles of Northumberland." Saren gestured toward the stranger, saying, "And this is my new friend, John Aston. And this, William, Pa, is my Nan."

The weak man took Mr. Aston's hand in a warm embrace and thanked him. "It wasn't I, my friend, but this lass who came all this way to see you to your freedom."

As they settled among the animals near the gate, Pa Wynch took Saren's free hand in his. "My girl, I thank ye.

But how did you manage it, I must ask?" He squeezed her small hand repeatedly.

"I owe my life to Ma Wynch and William. It was my pleasure, Pa. And I seldom did any of this on my own." Saren's smile warmed her soul from the inside.

"My dear girl, how on earth did you do it?" Pa Wynch, weak from hunger and cold, shivered as he crouched in the dirt.

"I know not, Pa Wynch. I simply believe the strength of my father's beautiful music amplified the storm that caused confusion and mayhem today. And I do know that we are escaping your execution—we remain criminals and, therefore, must run."

"True indeed, girl," Pa grumbled as he brushed his mouth with his sleeve. "The how matters not, My Lady," he corrected himself.

We cannot return home to London, Pa." Saren straightened her burdensome load. "The Church will be waiting for us there."

"Home, I long for home, as most would by now in my shoes. Or lack of." Pa chuckled, looking down at his tender, shoeless feet.

"I shall return to London alone and fetch Ma Wynch," Mr. Aston offered.

"Are we to remain here in this dreadful Oxford?" Pa's voice cracked in frustration.

"No, Pa." Saren retrieved her sacred book from beneath her belt. "We will not remain here. Together, we will take these sacred exposés abroad—we all will, together." Saren sighed as she cast her gaze on William.

Saren sat upon her haunches; her hand that held the worn book trembled. The silence about the group echoed fiercer than the raging storm beyond their hiding place.

Playing as the wind made Pa Wynch's rescue a success, Charles felt warmth for the first time across his countless days wandering. He continued to play and fill his bellows, though the tone and the chatter fell quiet beyond the wind's rage. He stepped deliberately and confidently into the warm glow of heavenly light that consumed him.

The winds beyond the stone wall ceased nearly as rapidly as they had started. Tucking the sacred book beneath her tunic, Saren and her companions stood together and left the shelter of the city's walls.

"Egypt is where the books should be delivered? Away, the books must be taken far away and protected. The sacred words must be kept secret, for this world is not yet ready to know what secrets are to be revealed." Saren caught her breath. "I have transcribed some of the books from Coptic." Saren stood as she explained, "There is a good and a bad to all things, all people." She sighed. "I carry the fifth, sixth, and seventh pieces of the Gospel of Mary. The others remain lost." Saren knelt near Nan saying, "The

Sophia of Jesus Christ explains that the ordering is directed in three ways by the philosophers, hence they do not agree. For some of them say about the world that it is directed by itself. Others, that it is providence. Others that it is fate. But it is none of these. Again, of the three voices mentioned. None is close to the truth, as they are from man. . . Jesus speaks of the precise nature of truth for whatever is from itself is a polluted life; it is self-made. Providence has no wisdom in it. And fate does not discern." [5]

Pa coughed quietly, drawing Saren's full attention to his worsening condition.

"Nan, The Holy One says in The Sophia of Jesus Christ that 'To you it is given to know; and whoever is worthy of knowledge will receive it. Now first begotten is called 'Christ'. Since he has authority from his father, he created a multitude of angels without number for retinue from Spirit and Light. All who come into the world, like a drop from the Light, are sent by him to the world of Almighty, that they might be guarded by him.'"[6]

Looking to Pa Wynch, Saren exclaimed, "We must go away at once, as far as your legs will carry you today. When you are well, we will move again. Mr. Aston will return to London for Ma Wynch, and we will meet again at Old Portsmouth. From there, together, we will travel to Egypt. There, we will find further translations of these Coptic treasures and transcribe them for safekeeping. The world as we know it is not ready to accept such truths. Above all, this wisdom must be protected from destruction while we hide and uncover the hidden truths hidden within the ancient Coptic text."

Pa stood taller with his new freedom.

Saren's smile filled her heart. "Yes, Captain Joseph's gift of a Coptic Bible has served me well. Now is the time to flee to Alexandria and learn all we can of the meanings lost in my Coptic translations together. There shall be no carrying this burden alone. Nor has there ever been, Saren remembered the Lord's words from her translations, 'Lord Savior, how many are the aeons of those who surpass the heavens?' and the perfect Savior replying, 'I praise you because you ask about the great aeons, for your roots are in the infinities.'[7]"

*　　*　　*

A note from Ondi Laure

The gift given in the Gnostic Bibles is that we are Christ/ Sophia within, made in his/her likeness, and capable of the same awareness and resonance. We are made of one blood, one Father, one Mother, consciously connected: one.

Our mission is then to overcome and break free, or tame and lasso, the human egoic mind and break free from the destructive cycle of mediocrity. We must shift our conscious thinking beyond our limited patterns of belief and into a Christlike existence (Heaven on Earth) as was intended by the Creator.

Intentionally creating the greatest impact with the Morningstar Series, life today mustn't wait for the conscious collective to catch up and align. As Saren chooses to explore beyond her comfort levels and entertain her father's primitive egoic mind, a similar journey, Mary Magdalene, embarked on, a journey of divination inward with the divine. The journey inward is unique to every soul. We are co-creating journeys of manifestation, either consciously or unconsciously.

I invite you to join our voices in conversation and in
a song about the Morningstar series: https://www.
facebook.com/groups/booksforgirls

Cited Sources

1 Gnosis.org/library/marygosp.html

2, 3 Luminarium. Anthology of English Literature, "The Ballad of Chevy Chase." http://www.luminarium.org/medlit/medlyric/chevychase.htm

4, aprocophonhohn.html

5,6,7 Parrott, Douglas M. *The Sophia of Jesus Christ.* 2001-2020. The Sophia of Jesus Christ hppt://www.earlychirstianwritings.com/text/Sophia.html